# LIVIN' AIN'T EASY

# *LIVIN' AIN'T EASY*

*PÉRON LONG*

**www.urbanbooks.net**

Urban Books
1199 Straight Path
West Babylon, NY 11704



ISBN- 13: 978-1-60162-143-6
ISBN- 10: 1-60162-143-4

First Printing March 2009
Printed in the United States of America

10 9 8 7 6 5 4 3 2 1

Distributed by Kensington Publishing Corp.
Submit Wholesale Orders to:
Kensington Publishing Corp.
C/O Penguin Group (USA) Inc.
Attention: Order Processing
405 Murray Hill Parkway
East Rutherford, NJ 07073-2316
Phone: 1-800-526-0275
Fax: 1-800-227-9604

## Acknowledgments

First and foremost I am thankful to God for the gift of written word that He chose to bless me with.

My parents, Paul and Helen Long, your love and support throughout my life is nothing but pure love, and I thank God for allowing me to be your son. Paul Long, Jr., my big "bruddah," thanks for always being by my side. Granny and Pop, thanks for the foundation. Kristen Scott, thanks for all the support. We are truly about to do some big thangs! To Peyden, I appreciate you more than words can express! Al and Tamala Boyd, thanks a million for the love and support! Monica Rivers, you have definitely been my lifesaver over the past few years. . . . Thanks! The Crew: B.R. Wilson, Wade Witherspoon III, Josephine "Jo Dog" Dogan, Sandra Calhoun-White, thank you for the fellowship! Jimiko "Miko Wiko" Witherspoon, thank you for being my good "buddy." Terry and Christy Lewis—love you two; thanks for being family. The Gethsemane Church family, thanks for the support, even though some of you say I write too nasty. Ha-ha. John Sutton, man, you know you my main dog! Thanks for the processing when it's needed. The fellas: Bunny, Derrick, Mario, DeMario, Darren, Chuck, and Stacey, thanks for keeping me grounded.

To all the authors I've met and become close friends with over the years, I thank you much for all the advice and support given. Dwayne S. Joseph, man, I really appreciate all that you've done to help me in my journey. Your support has been wonderful, and I am looking forward to all that "fun" you keep telling me about! LOL Portia, Cannon, I appreciate all you've done, as well as the patience you've shown me. Thanks a million! To Aisha Moore, I really appreciate all of your help and look forward to reading all of your work in the near future. To Carl Weber and the Urban Books family, I thank you for this opportunity and I'm looking forward to a great relationship. Sheila, you know you are nothing but a "Jewel." Thanks for all you've done and the wonderful friendship. D.L. Sparks, my literary twin, you are now on and about to be poppin! LOL Tina Brooks McKinney, my literary aunt, you have done so much and I appreciate you dearly. To all my MySpace friends, thanks for all the love shown! Continue to keep that love flowing!

To *everyone* I have crossed paths with, for whatever reasons God has placed us in one another's lives, I'm sure it was for greatness to come from it. I love you all, even if your name doesn't appear!

Thanks and I hope you enjoy!

Péron F. Long

Peron1@peronflong.com
www.peronflong.com
www.myspace.com/lilsouthernboy36

# *Prologue*

She hurried into the hotel room, threw her suitcase on the bed, unzipped it, and removed the clothes that were neatly folded inside. After taking off the long T-shirt and baggy jeans she had been wearing for what seemed like a lifetime, she removed one of the liners from the trash can next to the desk and stuffed the clothes inside. Then she walked into the bathroom to shower.

"What have I done?" she whispered, staring at her naked body in the mirror. "What have I become?"

After the shower she still felt no comfort, the thoughts of what had just happened playing repeatedly in her mind. It was hard to believe that she was capable of her actions.

She put on fresh clothes and walked over to the bed where her suitcase lay open. Two items remained inside. They both held the possibilities of her future. A future that was now uncertain. She had not planned what lay ahead, had not desired it, but had still created it. As she continued to stare at both items, her head felt as if it were going to explode. She forced herself to walk away from the bed and retrieve her pocketbook from where it had dropped on the floor. After retrieving two aspirin from her pocketbook, she popped them both into her mouth without any water. The dry pills felt stuck in her throat. She returned to the suitcase, again staring at the two items.

"Jamaica," she began softly to herself. "It's been a while since I've been there. I wonder if things are still the way I remember."

She selected one of the items from the suitcase, a one-way plane ticket, and sat on the edge of the bed, staring at it, remembering the times when she walked the beautiful beaches of the island, allowing the warm rays from the sun to dance upon her skin. She remembered the taste of exotic fruits that exploded inside her mouth. Those simple thoughts brought a smile to her face. Those simple thoughts did something she never realized could happen. They proved that she could enjoy the simpler things that life had to offer.

Her smile quickly became a frown as she glanced at the second item in the suitcase, the item that reminded her of the realities of her future. She tried to tear her eyes away from it, but the cold steel object seemed to speak to her, telling her that it carried her real future and that there was no other way.

A lone tear fell from her eye. She did not bother to wipe it. Her heart felt heavy, and the dry pills she took earlier seemed to expand in her throat, leaving a hard and unpleasant lump. She walked to the sink and used one of the cups that sat beside the towels. As she tore the plastic off, it clung to her hands, not wanting to let go.

"Why couldn't I just let go?" she asked herself, sipping the water.

She placed the plane ticket back into the suitcase beside the cold steel object, closed it, and set it on the floor in front of the bed. It was time to do something she had never done before. She needed to pray to God to forgive her.

# *Part I*

# 1

# *Devlin Carter*

When my eyes opened, I suddenly felt nervous. I was naked, and there was a naked woman beside me. I did not remember who she was. As I began to move around, she did too. I could still smell a slight hint of her perfume, and there was only one woman I knew who wore it: Leslie.

I looked over at the clock that sat on my dresser across the room. *Three-twenty-two AM* it read in big red numbers that illuminated the dark room. I replayed the entire evening in my head, but all I could remember was getting drunk then having an argument with her.

My mouth was dry, so I headed to the kitchen for a bottle of water. As the cold water refreshed my parched throat, I suddenly heard Leslie yell from my room.

"Goddamn it, why the hell didn't you wake me up?" She turned on the lamp beside my bed.

"I just woke up myself," I replied drily as I walked back to my room.

I climbed back in my bed just as she emerged from it, scrambling to collect all of her things. She reached for her pocketbook, grabbed her phone, and checked her voice mail.

"Shit, shit, shit, shit," she said softly to herself. "I can't believe let you let me fall asleep."

I didn't respond. To be honest, I could not remember what led either one of us into my bedroom. The last thing I remembered was the two of us sitting in my living room arguing while I took shot after shot of Crown Royal.

As I lay in my bed thinking about the past several hours, Leslie walked into the bathroom carrying all her belongings. In less than fifteen minutes, she came out looking exactly as she did when she arrived to my house the evening before.

"Bye," was all she said as she walked out of the room and out of my house.

After getting up and locking the door, I climbed back in bed and tried to replay as much of the events of the past ten hours as I could. Before any thoughts could form, sleep invaded my body once more.

I did not wake up until almost noon. I was somewhat frustrated because for the third time that month, I did not make it to church. I had made a promise to my grandmother that I would do my best to attend as often as I could.

"Don't you turn your back on the Lawd because things are going good for you," I could hear her voice echoing in my mind. "As quickly as God bless you with the things he gives you, he could take away just as fast."

Instead, I showered and headed to the grocery store to find something for dinner. On my way back home, my cell phone began to sing the assigned song telling me who was calling.

"What's up?" I asked.

"We need to talk," Leslie said after a brief silence.

"We did that last night. Remember?

I was really becoming irritated with all these "talks" that we had been having. They always seemed to end with us arguing, then having sex.

"Devlin," she started. "I know I've put you through some aggravating moments over the past few years, but I need you to know that it was never my intent to hurt you in any way. Lately I find myself thinking about you more than ever when we are not together, and when we are together I completely forget everything else that's going on in my life."

"Like your husband?" I asked, interrupting her.

"Yes," Leslie said softly, almost whispering.

Suddenly the night before replayed vividly. I remembered her asking me if I would take her back if she left her husband, Thomas. I remembered explaining to her that for five years, that's all she had been saying she was going to do, yet she was there with him.

I had even admitted to her that there was a time that I would have jumped at the chance for us to be together again. I honestly had a strong love for her, but now things were much different and the way I view her had changed tremendously.

Leslie and I met about six years ago at a cookout. I was immediately attracted to her. She wore her hair short and in natural waves. She was about five feet five and had a seriously toned body. Her skin was the color of a Hershey bar and her lips were full and luscious. I wanted her, and when our eyes met, I knew that she wanted me too.

At the time, I was a single middle-school teacher who was always trying to develop new teaching techniques to help my kids. She was a paralegal looking to marry someone with money. After finding out what I did for a living, and how little I made, she quickly moved me into the "friends" category, a place I stayed until she met and later married Thomas E. Jones III, attorney-at-law.

She would often call me and complain about how life with him was boring and the sex was horrible. I joked with her about being able to give her what she needed sexually. After months of filling her head with my desires, we began a sexual relationship that extended from the time she said yes to his marriage proposal until the present.

For five years, I fooled myself that our relationship was perfect because it was strictly sexual with no emotional ties. I tried convincing myself that a relationship like this was convenient and necessary.

Things changed when I quit my job teaching after eight years. I decided to devote my time to developing and selling educational products. I told myself that the situation with Leslie was perfect; I had someone to spend time with, and when I needed time to take care of business, I didn't have to worry about taking time away from my loved ones.

What took seven years to create and market had finally become a huge success. In the last six months my products made me a very wealthy, but still single, man. In addition, success brought relatives I never knew, friends I never had, and a love that suddenly wanted to be with me and me only.

It had taken me months, but I finally realized that the only true reason that she would leave him for me now was the sure fact that I could afford her.

"I love you," Leslie said, breaking into my thoughts.

"Leslie . . ." I paused for a few moments to gather myself. "I would be a liar if I told you that I didn't love you, because I do and I always will. But I am now realizing that just because I love you, doesn't mean that I have to be with you."

"Thomas just pulled up," she said after a brief silence and hung up without saying good-bye.

I pulled into my driveway and sat in my car for a few moments in deep thought. I asked myself if I truly loved her the way I thought I did, or was I in love with the convenience that came with her. She provided the physical satisfaction I craved, but I knew she could never offer me much more than that. I needed a woman that would be with me through any situation. After seeing how quickly she would leave her husband, after all of these years I sat in wait, I knew she could not be the type of woman I needed.

Walking into my house still wandering in my thoughts, I realized that my dealings with Leslie had cheated me out of several opportunities to be with women who would love me the way I desired. I wasted years hoping that one day she would be mine. I wasted years wishing that she would accept me for who I was. I spent years hoping that one day she would look beyond materialistic desires. But she never did, and now I felt like a fool for believing that she ever would. I was crazy to believe that she could.

I placed my groceries on the kitchen counter and walked back into my living room, where I sat on my couch. Leslie was not good for me. Continuing to deal with her would only lead to more heartache and pain. Even so, my heart still craved her. I still desired her.

# 2

# *Simone Jackson*

When I was a little girl, I used to fantasize about being rich and famous. I remember when I first saw Oprah Winfrey at the age of twelve and I would dream of one day taking her place. I dreamed of having my own Stedman, but unlike Oprah, I would marry him and have three kids. We would live the perfect life together and be one big, happy family. Now I was in my early thirties, and although part of my dream was a reality, the part I desired the most was still a dream. A dream that, due to my current situation, may never be a reality.

For the past three years, my talk show had been a local hit and a leader of its time slot. After months of being flirted by a couple of major networks, we were taking *An Afternoon with Simone Jackson* nationwide.

I was excited but at the same time terrified to death. Losing your privacy is the cost of fame, something I had been able to protect for years. I never understood why so many people seemed to care so much about my personal life.

I never thought I would be the interest of so many people in a small market like Charlotte, North Carolina. When

I arrived here in the mid-nineties, I was a reporter for one of the major news stations and before I knew it, I had my own weekly segment interviewing local people of interest. Then the talk show and all the sudden inquiries into my personal life.

The executive producer of my show—and my mentor—Suzette Jennings, would always ask me when I planned to settle down, and my only reply to her would be "one day." The truth was that I was already in a committed situation. I believed that my personal life outside of the show was mine to do damn well as I pleased. Whose business was it what I did? I was a grown-ass woman with the ability to do any and everything I desired.

Nevertheless, even though I felt settled, I still found myself sad and unhappy with my choice. I often found myself wondering whether I chose this life, or it chose me only to not let me go.

Most Sunday mornings I usually spent evaluating my life. Sundays were the only days I had for me and me alone. I stopped going to church years ago because every time I was there, the pastor made damn sure to remind me constantly that I was a sinner and that I was going to go to hell because of my sins. I got enough of that from my mother, who felt it was her mission to call me a thousand times a week to remind me of my sins.

"I don't care how much money and fame you get, your soul is going to burn in hell," she would always tell me. "You need to pray and ask God to deliver you."

I grew up in a small town in Alabama called Union Springs, about an hour outside of Montgomery. As a child, I was not exposed to much of anything except school and church. My father was a Baptist preacher, my mother was a teacher, and I was their one and only daughter.

My parents, mainly my mother, always stressed the importance of receiving an education, getting married, and having plenty of children—something they were unable to do after I was born. My mother truly thrived on tradition.

"When you find a good man like Steven, you hold on to him for life. Just like I did with your father," she would often tell me.

Steven Cole was the only boy my parents allowed me to date in high school. He was the son of one of the deacons at the church where my father was the pastor, and the love of my life until I was twenty-one.

After graduating high school, we both attended Auburn University in nearby Montgomery. Steven was a star basketball player, and I was his quiet, unsuspecting virgin and naive girlfriend.

My first year in college provided me with freedom from my parents, something I never thought I would have. It also gave me insight to things I had never before seen or experienced. To say that it was life-altering would be an understatement. There were so many things that I never knew existed in life. I love my parents with all my heart and I always believed they were excellent parents, but their decision to shelter me from the world hindered my growth.

My roommate, Carmen Rinehart, a slender, blond, blue-eyed girl from southern California, had a lifestyle that, up until meeting her, I had never been exposed to. One day, after spending hours in the school library working on a term paper, I came back into our dark room. She often stayed away, so I assumed she was not there. When I turned the light on, I saw her and one of her girlfriends lying across the bed, naked and asleep. I was so startled that I dropped everything I was carrying onto the floor, making so much noise that both of them jumped up.

Carmen initially looked embarrassed, but her friend gave me a sly smile followed by a long and seductive stare.

"If you are curious, I will be more than willing to ease

that curiosity for you," she said before she grabbed her clothes and went into our bathroom.

I had never been so nervous in all my life. I remembered my heart pounding so hard it felt as if it were going to jump out of my chest and run away.

Carmen grabbed her robe and walked over to me as she wrapped her robe around her slender body.

"Simone . . ." She paused as if she was trying to find the right words to say. "I did not mean for you to see us like this. She's usually gone before you come in, but I guess we were both tired and fell asleep."

I was speechless and in shock. After regaining the feelings in my legs, I walked toward my bed and sat down. As I sat on my bed with trembling hands, Carmen's friend came out of the bathroom. Carmen walked her to the door and they gave each other the most passionate kiss I had ever seen two people give each other in all my life. Once they separated from one another, Carmen's friend looked at me.

"I loves me some chocolate," she said, then winked at me and walked out the door as my heart began to pound again.

I had heard of lesbians before, but until then I had never actually known one. I was afraid to sleep at all that night. I kept wondering if Carmen would try to do anything to me while I slept.

When I finally got out of bed the next morning, I noticed that Carmen was gone. I immediately called Steven to tell him what had happened.

"Get out!" he yelled. "So did you watch them?"

"No, I didn't watch them!" I shouted.

For some reason, that question annoyed the hell out of me. Why would he even think that I would want to see that? I had never seen a woman's naked body before, other than in movies, in all my life.

After hanging up with Steven, I showered and headed to class. But the entire day, the only thing that was on my mind was the image of Carmen and her friend kissing. The passion they had was something that seemed so unreal. As often as Steven and I kissed, I don't think that either one of us had ever shown that much passion before.

Later that evening, instead of going to the library, I decided to study in my room. After sitting at my desk for over an hour trying to concentrate, there was a knock on the door. Carmen jumped off her bed and quickly walked to the door and opened it. It was her friend. As soon as she walked in, they began kissing. They were all over each other, not caring at all that I was there.

I attempted several times to ignore them but, for whatever reason, I found it hard not to look at the two of them. This was something new to me. As I stared at them, I realized that I had begun to study them more than my book that sat directly in front of me. I was intrigued by the way she touched Carmen. I was enthralled at the way Carmen accepted her touches. However, more than anything, I was mesmerized by her friend's body.

She had long brown hair and a tan from head to toe, making her look almost golden. After watching them nonstop for about twenty minutes, I decided it was time for me to leave. As I was gathering my things, I looked over and noticed Carmen's friend was staring at me while she was passionate with Carmen. This time my heart did not pound. I was not nervous. I began to get a different feeling. I became aroused. I quickly left.

Carmen and I remained roommates until my senior year when I moved off campus and into an apartment. The first semester of my senior year, on the night of my twenty-first birthday, I finally lost my virginity to Steven.

As much as I loved him, I hated to admit that what we

shared was the worst sexual experience I had ever imagined. The next night Carmen came over and I told her about my experience with Steven. She began laughing while we were sitting on my couch, drinking wine. She told me of her first sexual experience with a man when she was sixteen, and her second experience the next night with a woman. After the woman, Carmen had never been with or desired another man since.

I went on to tell her about our first year when I saw her and her friend kissing and the passion that they had.

"Would you like to experience that same passion?" she asked seductively.

Before I could say a word, her lips touched mine, and it was like nothing I could have imagined. She knew exactly what to do to make me feel wonderful. My heart began to pound, but it was not because I was nervous. My nipples felt as if they were going to explode, and my sweetness was as wet as ever.

She tickled my neck with her tongue, knowing exactly what to do. Her touch felt soft and sensuous. I lay there on the couch, not moving a muscle and allowing passion to invade my body. Carmen's tongue touched every part of my aroused body. Once she arrived at my sweetness, I exploded, but she did not budge. She continued to taste me, making me flow like a never-ending stream.

Once she finished, she did not say a word. Carmen simply got up, put on her shoes, and then walked to the door. Before walking out, she looked back and smiled.

"If you ever want to go farther than what just happened, call me," she said, leaving me lying on the couch still having an orgasm. Within twenty minutes, Steven became a distant past, and I became the devil's daughter in my mother's eyes.

# 3

# *Devlin*

After eating Sunday dinner, I lay on my couch to watch a game but eventually fell asleep. Since my early retirement, it seemed as if all I did most afternoons—most days, actually—was sleep.

When I was a senior in college, it was my dream to be able to retire by the time I turned thirty-five. I told myself that the first thing I would do is take my wife on trips around the world. Buy her the biggest house she ever wanted. I even said that I would buy my grandmother, who raised me since I was a baby, any and everything that she wanted.

Six months ago, when American Educational Incorporated, one of the largest suppliers of educational products, bought my products, it provided me with money for four lifetimes.

I reached my retirement goal three years early to find myself all alone in the world. The one woman I ever really loved was never and could never be mine, and my grandmother died four years ago only to see me still struggling.

* * *

I never bought the big house I wanted for my make-believe wife. I still lived in the two-bedroom house that my grandmother left me when she died. I did some traveling, but only to promote the products that I created. Other than that, I spent most of my days at home, wishing I were back in a classroom teaching.

When I finally got up from my nap, I called my best friend since elementary school. Jacob Brown was the closest thing I ever had to a brother or even a cousin. My parents were never a part of my life. My mother died when I was only two, and I never met or even knew who my father was.

Jacob's family had moved down the street when we were both in third grade. He was actually three months younger than I, but he was much bigger.

"He be big-boneded because he mama be big-boneded," I could still hear Grammy say.

Jacob was always my protector. All the other kids were naturally afraid of him because of his size, and he looked as if he had a frown on his face even when he laughed. Jacob was a light-skinned brother with naturally curly hair, traits that all the girls loved back then. By the time we got to high school, his big size began to take the shape of pure muscle and he became a star football player, a talent that landed him a college scholarship and the opportunity to play professional football.

Renal failure ended his career after five years in the league. After his body rejected two kidneys, he was forced to live off a dialysis machine and his muscular frame had faded away. I did not go visit as often as I should or as much as I wanted. It was hard seeing how the disease had reduced him.

"Hello," the drained voiced said into the phone.

"We are climbing Jacob's Ladder . . . We are climbing Jacob's Ladder," I sang into the phone.

I heard him give a faint laugh.

"What up, fool?" he finally responded.

"Not too much; fell asleep watching your boys get their asses kicked," I told him, referring to the Carolina Cougars, the last team he played for before he got sick.

"Yeah, I fell asleep too. So what's on your plate for the rest of the day?"

"That's why I called you," I began. "I was thinking about heading over to your place. Are the wife and kids there?"

There was a pause. It sounded as if he was trying to catch his breath.

"Yeah, they're here, and we'd love for you to drop by. It'll be good to see you, Mr. Trump," he said as he gave that faint laugh again before hanging up.

I went to my room to get my shoes when my cell phone rang, singing the familiar ringtone.

*Leslie.*

I hit the ignore button, put on my shoes, and headed out the door to visit my friend.

Once I arrived, Jacob's two boys were outside tossing the football. His oldest son, Jacob Jr., who we call Li'l J, was eleven and already as tall as me. His younger son, Cody, was nine.

"Li'l J, you're as tall as me now, man," I said as he threw the football toward me.

"Uncle Dev, it doesn't take much to be as tall as you," he said laughing.

As I walked toward the front door, I looked back at the boys, thinking about how much both of them had grown. Li'l J was already five feet eight, only an inch shorter than I was. When I was his age, I was barely five feet two, and Cody was taller than that at nine.

After knocking one time on the door, I walked in. I heard Jacob's wife, Stephanie, in the kitchen. She was still as beautiful as ever. The first time he introduced me to her, I thought she was a black goddess.

Her hair was long and smooth and her skin was like pure chocolate. She stood about five feet five. In college, she ran track, and she continued to stay in shape.

When I got closer, she looked up and seemed to be surprised to see me.

"Hey, Dev, I didn't hear you come in," she said, wiping her hands on a towel as she walked toward me to give me a hug.

The hug was longer than normal. When she released from our embrace, I saw a stream of tears flowing down her face. I took a seat on one of the stools at the center island counter in the middle of the kitchen. Her tears told me everything.

As she sat on the other side of the counter, there was a long moment of silence.

"Want a beer?" she asked after wiping the tears away.

"Sure," I whispered.

The silence continued. It spoke in more detail what her tears had just told me, but I was afraid to ask, and I did not want her to tell.

"Jacob is upstairs in his hideaway room," she said as she placed the beer in front of me.

I did not say another word. I grabbed my beer and headed upstairs.

I was always amazed at Jacob and Stephanie's house. It reminded me of the house I wanted to give my grandmother or the woman that lived in my mind.

Jacob and Stephanie had a pure love that only heaven could have made. They met when they were freshmen in college, and after he made it to the pros, they were married. He wasted no time in providing those that he loved everything they wanted or the things he just wanted them to have.

Jacob was able to do at an early age the things that were always my dream to do, a dream that is now a reality. A reality in which I am alone.

As I got closer to the room he called his hideaway, I remembered when he had the plans for this house drawn. He included a room only for him and his friends. No wives or kids allowed. The first time I walked into the hideaway, my only thought was how this one room was larger than Grammy's house and Jacob's parents' house combined.

When I walked in the room, Jacob was wearing a housecoat and sitting in his recliner by the window, looking out at his boys throwing the football. He had a look of sorrow written all over his face. I stared at him for a few moments as he watched his sons. I could tell that he wished he could be out there with them.

"What up?" I said, trying to hide the feelings of my own sadness.

When he looked my way, a huge smile came across his face.

"Dev," he said softly. "I thought I saw your raggedy-ass car pull up," he said and then began to laugh.

"How are you feeling?" I could tell that it was a bad day and felt a little uneasy for asking him that question.

"Every day I'm above ground, I thank God for His grace and His mercy," he said after taking a slow sip of water from the cup that sat on the stand beside him.

"Amen," I replied.

As we sat and talked for hours, I felt like crying several times. Jacob was a man that had dominated the football field. He would hit people so hard that he could knock them into another year. Renal failure had left him only a shell of what he once was. I had never seen Jacob so small and it made me sad.

Over the years, I saw my friend's health decline and I watched him as he died slowly. Being on dialysis made his skin darker and older than what he was. This was new to me. When Grammy died, it was a heart attack, sudden. Not lingering like this.

"I saw you on *Good Morning America* last week," he said, breaking me out of my thoughts.

"You did? Did I look crazy?" I asked, smiling.

"Negro, man, you always look crazy to me." He laughed and began to cough uncontrollably.

When I got up to walk toward him, he held his hand up to let me know that everything was okay. When I sat back down, there was a long silence. There was so much that I wanted to say, but my emotions had the best of me.

"I'm going to be on Simone Jackson's show this week," I said, trying to create conversation.

"Make sure you let me know so I can check you out." He paused. "That's one fine sister. She interviewed me when I first found out I was sick. There was something different about her, though. I never could pinpoint it."

More silence. We both had so much to say, yet it seemed as if we were unsure of how to say it.

"You know what song has been playing in my head the past few days?" he asked, breaking our silence.

"Public Enemy's 'Fight the Power'?" I replied, remembering after seeing the movie *Do the Right Thing*, for weeks that was the only song he would play in his CD player.

"Nah, not that one, but you do have to admit it's a classic." We both laughed. "The song that's been playing in my mind is the one your grammy played every single day."

I felt my eyes fill with tears.

"James Cleveland . . . 'No Ways Tired'," I whispered. We continued to sit in silence for twenty more minutes when Stephanie came into the room.

"The nurse is here, baby," she told him.

That was my cue to leave. I walked over to my friend and gave him a hug. As I began to walk out, he stopped me.

"Dev, you are worth millions of dollars now. It is 2009. Why are you still driving that raggedy-ass '94 Lexus?" he asked, smiling.

"Sentimental reasons," I said as I reached the door to the room. I turned around to continue. "My best friend gave it to me when he made it to the pros."

# 4

# *Simone*

My Sunday afternoon ritual usually consisted of take-out from Down to the Bone and going over my shows of the week.

Ever since I could remember, I had been a stickler for detail. I always wanted to be sure that I was on top of my game. I read every available bit of information about my guests. This method, although tedious, was very important in understanding people and having the best show possible. Sometimes the information nearly put me to sleep, but on some rare occasions I would find a guest that intrigued me.

It was around six PM when I finished my research. The next part of my ritual was to grab a bottle of wine out of the fridge, pop some popcorn, and sit on the floor in front of my plasma to watch *Love Jones*, one of my favorite movies of all time.

Every time I watched it, I cried. Not because of the love found, love lost, love found again theme, but because deep down inside, I knew I wanted a Darius Lovehall of my own. That particular Sunday was at least my two-hundredth time watching it, but I still cried as if it were the first. As soon as the movie started and I heard Dionne sing the chorus, tears began to flow uncontrollably.

It was a song that would always invade my mind with questions. Am I hopeless? Am I no less? Am I up to my head in it?

Before my first year in college, I was never aware of my attraction toward women. It took me years to act on it, but when I first saw Carmen and her friend in our room, I realized I had an attraction. For whatever reason, seeing them aroused me, and at the time it felt natural, even though somewhere deep down I knew that the feeling was not.

For years, I struggled with my sexuality. Even though my first love, Steven, was the only man that I had ever been with sexually, I still found myself attracted to men, yet I never acted on that attraction.

It eluded me why I chose to be in relationships with women. I had never been in love with any of them, and because I had always longed for a "traditional" family, I seriously doubted that I could ever be in love with a woman. I constantly found myself battling to understand why I continued to deal in a lifestyle that never brought me anything positive.

My choice of lifestyle had not gained me a thing. Even if I did fall in love with a woman, I knew that I could never be open about it. I never felt comfortable being intimate in public with another woman.

Last year when Trinity, my current partner, and I went to France, she would grab my hand as we took evening strolls through the city. I would allow this to go on for a few short minutes, but then I would point to something meaningless to regain my hand. It just felt uncomfortable and it seemed as if everyone had their eyes on us.

Because I was in the public eye, I was often concerned

about how the public saw me. Although my show was scheduled for syndication, it would be taped in Charlotte, and people in the South lived and breathed on "traditional" lifestyles.

Trinity often told me that I put too much emphasis on what people used to think about lesbians, and that it was now a more acceptable lifestyle.

"Look at Ellen," I remembered her saying one night in her strong Jamaican accent. "She is accepted, and you know how many people watch her show? Millions watch her show and love her."

I guess I looked more at the negative than I did the positive about life, and all I could see in my current life were the things that I felt that I lost. When I thought of my losses of living this lifestyle, I was more than aware that they outweighed the gains.

I lost what was once a decent relationship with my mother, and although my father never said anything to me about my decision, I could always see the hurt in his eyes.

I was twenty-eight years old when I broke the news to them, and the way it happened was an accident. My mom was hounding me about starting a family and after years of her aggravation, I blurted it out.

"I just can't understand," my mother said, crying, when I told her. "Your father and I raised you right. What happened?"

Since that day, my relationship with my mother had been minimal. The only times she called now was on Sunday mornings when she urged me to go to church and repent.

After Darius and Nina kissed in the rain, I hit the off button on the remote and started to clean up the pile of work I left on the floor. A picture of the upcoming guest who intrigued me fell from the stack to the floor. Devlin Carter.

I put everything on my dining room table, then came back to get the picture. For some reason, I could not tear my eyes from him. He was very attractive. About the color of cocoa before you mix it in milk. His hair was short and wavy and his eyes were hazel, and very hypnotic.

I had interviewed several men over the years who I found to be attractive, but no one intrigued me the way that this man did. I walked back to the table to get the folder with his information in it and sat back on the floor. As I reread it, it seemed as if I learned even more about this man. More than what was in the information I had, which was very little.

He was a middle-school teacher who created a line of educational products that many school districts across the nation were now using. Moreover, he was single.

"Why is an attractive, wealthy man such as yourself single?" I asked his picture aloud, as if it could answer me.

I continued looking at his eyes. I saw something different from what I saw in most people. He seemed to be compassionate. He appeared to be affectionate. But there was something else. I kept staring at the picture and his eyes. His eyes said that he was missing someone or something. His eyes looked as if he was missing what I felt I was missing.

"Could you be my Darius Lovehall?" I asked his picture.

Snapping out of my daze, I headed for bed. It was already ten o'clock and past my bedtime. But Devlin Carter was still walking through my mind, making it difficult for me to go to sleep.

"Why?" I asked aloud.

I was unable to sleep and my mind stayed on a man I had never met. It was crazy. I felt like I was back in high school and I had an uncontrollable crush on the most popular person in school.

*Ring . . . ring.*

The phone startled me. I looked at the caller ID before answering

*Unavailable.*

"Hello," I growled into the phone, mad as hell. I knew who it was, and I was mad that she had interrupted my thoughts.

"Hello, sweet love," the Jamaican-accented voice said.

"Trinity, how many times do I have to remind you that you are three hours behind me?" I was more pissed at her timing than I was the actual call.

"I'm sorry, love. I just left a shoot and bothered not to look at the time."

Trinity and I had been together for almost five years. We met in LA, where we both attended the NAACP Image Awards. After the show, we ended up at the same after party. The party was a bit boring to me, so I decided to leave. I was on my way out the door and to my room when she approached me.

"I saw you earlier tonight at the banquet and I think that you have the most luscious lips," she said, catching me somewhat off guard with that comment.

It always amused me how women from other countries showed no inhibitions on approaching someone that they were interested in, whether male or female.

Along with her complexion of smooth honey, tall slim figure, and long, silky jet-black hair, her boldness was something that turned me on completely.

"Would you like to leave and join me for a drink in my quarters?" she asked without an ounce of shyness in her composure.

"What makes you think that I would want to join you?" I asked.

"I just know," she said with a sly grin.

It was something about her accent and her boldness that made me tingle and made me say yes.

Once we arrived at her room, we sat in the sitting area, drank wine, and talked all night as if we were two old friends.

Her father was originally from London and her mother Jamaica. She was born in Jamaica and lived there until she was sixteen, when she and her parents moved to London. She came to the States at the age of seventeen to study fashion at NYU, and after graduating, she went to work in France with a company that she had interned with while in college. Trinity had so much passion for her job as a stylist, which turned me on too.

"I just called to inform you that my plane will arrive in Charlotte at ten AM. I know you will be taping, so I will hire a service to drop me at your place."

I had forgotten all about the banquet I was speaking at this upcoming Saturday. After her reminder, my initial thought was to tell her to stay where she was. But not only was she my lover, she was also my stylist.

After hanging up, my thoughts returned to Devlin Carter.

"Could you be my Darius Lovehall?" I asked again aloud.

# 5

## *Devlin*

On my way home from Jacob's house, the thought of my dying friend ran rapidly through my head. Everyone of any true significance in my life had left this earth.

My mother, whom I never got the chance to know; my grandmother, who raised me; and now my best friend—my brother—would soon leave. To say that I felt angry with God was a mild way to put it. I felt furious with Him. If He were as merciful as everyone says He is, why would He take those I love dearly? Why would He want to leave me in this world alone?

As my angry thoughts continued, my phone chimed.

*Leslie.*

She had already called six times and left six messages.

"What's up, Les?" I asked, somewhat pissed at her persistence.

There was a pause. "The question is, what's up with you?" she asked.

"Not much. Just left Jacob's."

"Are you almost home? I'm here at your house waiting on you."

*Damn!* I said to myself. I really was not in the mood for her today.

It was amazing that over the past few months she had found a lot of free time to be with me. In our five-year relationship, I was lucky if I saw her once a month. Now it was almost a daily thing, something I knew I had to end faster than soon.

When I turned the corner to my street, I noticed she was sitting in her car in my driveway, which meant that I had to park my car on the street. When she saw me, she got out of the car and met me at the front door.

"When are you going to buy a new car and house? You can afford anything you want. You do realize that you deserve better, don't you?" she asked as I ignored her, put my key into the lock, and walked in.

I placed my keys on the small table beside my front door and walked to the kitchen to grab a beer. She took a seat on the couch.

"I will have my realtor call you. She can find something really nice that we both would love," she rambled, getting up from the couch and blocking my path to reenter the living room.

"Are you listening to me? You are in a new tax bracket now. You don't have to live like this anymore."

I remained quiet, staring at her. She moved out of the way and returned to her seat on the couch while I sat in the chair across the room. She picked up the remote, turned the TV on, and began flipping the channels.

I remembered that I left something in my car. Without saying a word, I walked out of the house and returned with a pack of cigarettes. As I sat down, I took one out and placed it in my mouth.

"I know you are not about to light that thing in here," she said as a frown came over her face. "Besides, I thought you quit."

"I started back."

"And when did you start again?" Leslie asked.

"Twenty minutes ago, when you called to tell me you were sitting in my yard waiting on me."

There was a long and disturbing silence between us.

"How's Jacob?" she asked.

"Do you really care? The first thing you said to me when I got here was something about deserving a better house and car. Now you want to ask about my sick friend?"

"Would you like me to leave, Devlin? I didn't come over here to argue," she said as she reached for her purse.

I took a sip of my beer before I responded. "So why did you come? So that you can get a damn good nut before you go home to your husband?"

She gave a look of sadness, then stood up from the couch, grabbed her purse, and walked toward the door.

"I'm leaving," she said softly.

"Bye," I said, without looking up.

Leslie stopped at the door and looked back. We caught each other's eyes. I noticed hers watering.

"Why are you doing this now?" Leslie asked.

"You did say I deserved better, right?"

She walked out, understanding that what took me five years to do had just happened in a matter of minutes.

After she left, I went to the pantry and grabbed the bottle of Crown and a glass. I went back to the living room, lit a cigarette, poured the glass full, and began to drink and smoke my anger, sadness, and loneliness away.

"What are you trying to tell me, God?" I yelled aloud.

I always felt that during my sorrow God was speaking to me, but I could never understand what he was saying.

If Grammy were here now, she would direct me to a passage of scripture to read that would comfort me. She would say a positive word that would assure me that everything was going to be all right. But she was not here, and I had not felt that comfort since she died.

I woke up the next morning still on the couch. I looked at my watch that sat on the coffee table in front of the couch.

Seven-fifteen AM.

As I stumbled to the bathroom, my phone rang. It was my business manager, Billy Langston. He was a stubby white man in his late thirties.

"What's going on, buddy?" he asked cheerfully.

I could never understand how he always sounded so happy so early in the morning.

"I'm having a slight hangover," I responded.

He began to laugh uncontrollably.

"Just calling to let you know I'm about to fax this week's itinerary to you. Make sure you review it, and if you have any questions, you know what to do."

After hanging up with Billy and using the bathroom, I made it to my bedroom, where I keep the fax machine. Once the document was complete, I scanned it. There was only one appearance all week. *An Afternoon with Simone Jackson.*

"Why the hell did he fax this to me?" I asked aloud. "This was something he could have told me over the phone."

After taking a shower, I walked around the house with nothing but a towel on, trying to figure out what in hell I was going to do for the day. I missed the classroom. Most of all, I missed watching the excitement in the eyes of children when they learned something new. Over the past few months, I often wondered why I believed rich people had the best lives in the world; now here I was wishing I was getting up to go to work every day.

* * *

After throwing on a T-shirt and a pair of sweatpants, I fixed breakfast and ate and then decided to lie down again. It was nine-thirty and I was still feeling the hangover.

About one o'clock, I woke up. As I sat up on the couch, I glanced over at the TV that had been on all night. When my eyes finally adjusted, I saw the woman who would be interviewing me in three days, Simone Jackson.

This was my first time really paying any attention to her beauty. To be honest, it had been about five years since I really paid attention to any woman other than Leslie.

Simone was a smooth, dark-chocolate sister with some very exotic features. Her eyes were almond-shaped and she had some of the fullest lips I had ever seen on a woman. She could not have been more than five feet six or seven and not over 130 pounds, and not one ounce of that weight appeared to be fat.

As I watched her show, I found myself being completely curious about her, but not fully understanding why. Her voice was soft, yet heavy enough to command your full attention.

After her show, I decided to leave the house to go for a ride. There was a knock at my door as I put on my shoes.

I looked in the peephole. It was my grandmother's best friend, Betty Simpson. They had been friends for over forty years and had talked practically every day, until the day Grammy died. Ms. Betty missed Grammy as much as I did and would often stop by to bring me a cake or something to eat.

She asked how I was doing as she walked in with a plate covered with foil paper in her hand.

"I'm doing great, Ms. Betty," I said, reaching for the plate and giving her a kiss on her cheek.

Ms. Betty's children and grandchildren all lived out of state and seldom came to visit her. She was pretty much like a second grandmother to me and treated me as if I were one of her own.

"I woke up this morning and your grammy was on my mind, so when I fixed me some dinner, I decided to make some extra and walk over here to give it to you."

"Thank you. It's more than appreciated, Ms. Betty," I said as I took the plate to the kitchen.

When I returned to the living room, she had already taken a seat on the chair near the door and began smiling while looking around the house.

"You keeping up Essie's house real good, chile. She was so proud of you, and I know if she was still here, she would be more proud." She paused and took a long breath. "I was watching that pretty black girl who got that show. I heard her say your name and that you would be on there later this week." She paused again and closed her eyes. "Now what is that chile's name?"

"Simone Jackson," I answered.

"That's it, baby. Betty's mind getting old." She giggled. "I watch that chile every day and I still forgets her name. She sho' is a pretty and black thang, ain't she? Back in my day, a black person that dark would never be on TV." She laughed again, then stood up. "Well, I'm not going to worry your patience any longer, baby. I just want you to know you still loved."

"I love you too, Ms. Betty."

As she walked out of the house, I asked if she wanted me to drive her back home. She turned around and looked at me, smiling.

"No baby, I be fine. It is a beautiful day and I feels like walking and remembering my old friend. I sho' do miss that woman." A look of concern came over her face. "Speaking of friends, how is that Brown boy doing?" she asked, referring to Jacob.

It was always amusing to me when the elderly referred to people by their last names.

"He's not doing too well, Ms. Betty," I said sadly.

I saw a look of sadness come over her face. She walked back toward the steps where I was standing and grabbed both of my hands.

"Living ain't easy, chile, and it's even harder when those you love go on to meet the Lawd. You be strong, you hear me? You spend as much time with that boy while he still be here." She then hugged me and walked away.

I sat on the front porch and watched her as she walked away. I thought about all the years they spent together as friends and how they often argued with one another as if they were sisters. As she disappeared, I continued to reminisce about how close she and Grammy were and how, after Grammy died, it seemed as if part of her died too. Just like watching Jacob dying was causing pieces of me to die as well.

# 6

## *Simone*

"Damn, five AM comes quick as hell," I said as I hit the off button on the alarm clock on the table beside my bed.

Monday mornings always seemed to sneak up out of nowhere. It felt like I had only slept for five minutes. In addition, I had a slight hangover. I could not distinguish if it was from the whole bottle of wine that I had the night before or from all my crazy thoughts about a man I had never met.

While taking my shower, I thought about my past and my present. Where was my future heading?

I thought about Trinity and her desire to be in a serious relationship. She had repeatedly stressed it over the past year, and every time she brought it up, I gave her the same answer: That was not what I wanted from a woman.

"You git on my fock-ing nerves wit' tis shit, Simone!" Her Jamaican accent was always strong when she got mad. "You know you love me. You only tink what people would say if they knew you were wit' a wo-mon. You love me, Simone. Tell me you love me."

I never answered her. Yes, I cared for her, yet I did not love her the way she wanted me to. I knew that I could never love her the way she wanted me to. I did care what others thought of my personal life, but I also knew that my feelings about being committed to a woman had nothing to do with others. I had always known what I truly wanted.

What was becoming more evident was that my senior year in college, I became involved in a lifestyle that was only pleasurable. Who was to say that I could not find that same pleasure with a man? It's like I lived a lie for the last ten years of my life just because of one experience.

I arrived at the studio like clockwork at six-forty-five. I normally went over the script of the day, but this morning was different. This morning I sat at my desk and stared at nothing for over an hour.

"Good morning, sunshine," my executive producer, Suzette, said.

"Hey Suzette, how are you?" I said. "What's new?"

"Everything is new, sweet cheeks," she said with a huge smile on her face.

Suzette was a chubby, blond woman in her mid-fifties. She was well-proportioned for her size, and she always addressed people with cutesy names. When I first came to Charlotte, she was the executive producer of the news station that I worked at. I immediately fell in love with her, and I viewed her as my second mom.

"The network hired a publicist and she will be here this morning for the taping. After the show, we're having lunch and discussing your move to the big time," she said before taking a sip of coffee.

"Cool, looking forward to it," I said solemnly.

"Are you doing okay, bumpkins?" she asked, giving me a look of suspicion.

I smiled the best smile I could conjure up.

"Yeah, just a little tired, that's all."

Her look then became very serious. Her eyes pierced me as if she knew something without me telling her. She continued to stare at me silently while she took another sip of her coffee.

"Need to talk?" she asked.

I stared at her, and for some reason, my eyes began to water up. Before I knew it, I was crying like a baby. Suzette quickly ran over to me and hugged me.

"Sunshine, sunshine," she began as she held me. "What's wrong?"

"I don't know," I cried.

The sad thing about it was that I really did not know why I was crying. I just suddenly felt an overwhelming sensation of sadness.

"Do you want to postpone today's taping for an hour?"

I removed myself from her embrace, grabbed some tissue, and regained my composure.

"I'm okay. Just tired, that's all," I said, standing suddenly as if I were going somewhere, but then I just stood there in one spot.

"Simone," Suzette began as she grabbed my hand. "You are not crying because you're tired. Now tell Mama what's wrong."

Her smiles were contagious, and they always made me smile.

"Yesterday I did some life evaluations, and although I've accomplished a lot in the industry, my personal life is in shambles," I said after taking a long, deep breath and sitting back down behind my desk.

Suzette was the only person I felt comfortable confiding everything. She always seemed to understand me and never judged me, although she always stressed that I should be seen with a man every now and then.

"Suzette, I want so much more out of life. I am thirty-one, almost thirty-two years old, and I want to be a mother. Damn success, damn the fame, and damn money. I want a real family. The kind I had growing up." The tears reemerged and I began to bawl all over again.

This time Suzette did not walk over to hug me. She remained seated in the chair in front of my desk, sipping her coffee. After a few moments of silence, she stood.

"Sugar muffin, you know better than anyone that you can have any and everything you want. No one is holding you back from the real family you say you want but you. If you really want it, it's yours," she stated as she walked to the door and looked at her watch. "It is now eight-fifteen. I am pushing the taping to nine-thirty. I will send a production assistant in at nine-fifteen, okay?"

I nodded my head as she walked out the door. I was still sad, but for some reason I was beginning to feel a little bit better.

Suzette never stressed her personal opinions on how she felt about my situation, and she always listened to me without preaching, like my mother always did.

I began to think about my mother. Every time she crossed my mind, I felt a rush of rage.

Ever since I could remember, my mother's mission was to train me to be what she wanted. As a young girl, I had to be the perfect Southern belle.

"Sit up straight at all times. Pants are not for women. Always look presentable. What did you do to your hair? You look like a hussy." She would drive me crazy with her nagging.

When I was a senior in high school and I asked her about sex, she nearly knocked me into another century.

"Ladies do not discuss such nasty matters," she yelled as I lay on the floor of my room. "Never bring this up again. Do you understand me?"

"Yes, ma'am," I remembered saying as I lay there crying.

There was not a day that went by that that day did not cross my mind. Sometimes I felt that I chose to be with women to get back at my mother. But the only person that had truly been affected was me.

As much as I loved my mother, I sometimes hated her. I was never what she wanted me to be. She threatened to go on a hunger strike my junior year in college when I told her that I didn't want to teach. When I told her I was moving to Washington, D.C. after graduating college, she faked a heart attack to prolong my move. I lived in D.C. for about a year and a half and she never spoke to me the entire time I was there.

"That's the devil's playground, child. Why in the world would you want to live there?" she yelled. "You should come back home and stay with us. You can get a job at the school. Home is where you need to be until you and Steven get married." My only response was moving to D.C. to begin my life.

I had been at my desk, traveling down memory lane, when the production assistant informed me that I had fifteen minutes. As I walked toward the studio, I felt unprepared for the first time in my career.

I went back to my office after the show. I was pleased that I did not stumble nearly as bad as I thought I would. As I began to watch the playback of the show, there was a knock on my office door.

"Sweet cakes," Suzette said, walking in with a young black woman who appeared to be in her early to mid-twenties. "I want to introduce you to Charlene Humphries. She's your new publicist."

Charlene was a very attractive young woman. She was

about five feet four and the color of caramel. She wore short, neat golden dreads and looked somewhat artsy in jeans with tears at the bottom. She seemed to not care about what the world thought of her.

"Ms. Jackson, I would just like to say it's a pleasure to be working with you. I am so excited," she said as she and Suzette took seats in the chairs in front of my desk. We decided to order take-out and discuss our business relationship and expectations. For the first time all day, I felt focused and clear.

I arrived home around five that evening and immediately ran water in my tub for a long and hot bath full of bubbles. I stared at my body in the mirror as I stripped naked. I touched my flat stomach and imagined having another life growing inside me. What would it be like to have a man to share in that experience?

I climbed into the tub, turned on the whirlpool, and closed my eyes. As the water began to massage my body, the picture of Devlin Carter reappeared in my mind. My nipples hardened and my southern territory became moist, and it was not from the water swirling around me. I jumped out of the tub thinking that I had gone mad.

"How in the hell can I feel this way about a man I never met or even saw in person?" I said aloud.

It was around seven o'clock, and like every other night during the week, I relaxed in bed watching CNN until the television began to watch me. I wondered what Devlin was doing at that very moment. Was he thinking about being on my show? Was he with a woman, making her feel the way I felt in my tub? Maybe I was just going crazy.

"I think I need to see a psychiatrist," I whispered.

# 7
# *Devlin*

They say that a ménage à trois is every man's dream. There I sat with my two lovers in front of me, both of them saying the same thing to me at the same time.

*Devlin, Devlin. Come to us. Take us both in. You want us and we want you to have us.*

I sat on the couch in my living room in dim light, and the smooth, melodic sounds of George Duke poured from the CD player. I stared long and hard at my two lovers, not allowing myself to compare the two. They were both beautiful, and I desired them equally. I wanted them both. I craved them both. One was thick, bold, and as golden as the purest gold; the other slim, seductive, and whiter than fresh Christmas snow.

*Take me first*, said the white one, and I obeyed her command. I held her and stared at her a long time. I had been with her several times in the past, and had given her up only to invite her back in again.

I held her close to me and inhaled, letting her taste dwindle in my mouth. She was so sweet to me, but I knew she was no good for me, yet I still craved her. I released her, watching her aura dance around me, enticing me to take her in repeatedly.

While I held her slim white body in my hand, my golden love called me, persuading me to come to her.

*Now me, Devlin. Take me and do me as you did her.*

I listened to her. I was under her command.

I swallowed her quickly, repeatedly, until I was numb, until I no longer felt the pain in my heart, until my mind was far away from this world. Far away from the pain that had invaded me.

I met them both years ago, and since meeting them I grew to love and depend on them. They both soothed me. They both allowed my mind to rest, although their relief was only temporary.

The three of us remained intertwined for hours. They constantly called my name, commanding me to take them. I was their slave, and I did as they commanded until I finally passed out on the couch.

I woke up around three AM in a drunken stupor and looked over at my two lovers. My golden beauty was practically empty, and my white seductress's green and white package contained only one more of her slim sticks.

I sat up, looking at them while my head screamed for relief. I had not felt like this in ages. I knew when I started drinking earlier that evening that I would wake up with a huge hangover, but at the time, my only concern was to escape my hurt, even if it was only for a small period.

For years, liquor and cigarettes were my refuge. I hated the way I felt after indulging, but I also craved those feelings. Sometimes it seemed I could hear Grammy talking to me through my indulgence. I could still hear her giving me life lessons.

"Trust in God, chile. He will always be there for you," she

would always tell me. Sitting there with my head throbbing, Grammy's words replayed repeatedly in my mind, but they gave me no comfort. They gave my soul no ease.

I could never grasp the idea of trusting someone who had stolen so much from me; someone who had stolen dreams, love, and family. How could I depend on Him when He left me alone?

After wallowing in my sadness, I finally emerged from the couch and staggered into my bedroom. I pulled back the sheets and climbed in my bed. I listened to Thelonius playing his piano, and tears fell from my eyes. I felt a strong pain pierce my heart until I finally fell asleep.

I woke up the next morning around ten. My head still throbbed, but not as badly as earlier. I stumbled, walking to the kitchen to make a pot of coffee. After pouring the strong-smelling substance in a cup, I walked back to my room, sat on the bed, and then turned on the TV. As I flipped through the channels, my home phone rang. I glanced at the caller ID.

*Leslie.*

I let the phone ring until voice mail picked up. I couldn't talk to her. If I had, she would be on her way over and I would make love to her as if she were my woman, only to have her leave and go home to her husband.

As much as I tried to deny my feelings for her, they continued to remain embedded in my heart. The more I tried to tell her we were over, she somehow heard my heart telling her something very different. Why did I love her? Why did I crave her? Why was she on my mind every time I went on a date with another woman?

I drank my coffee and continued flipping through the channels. The phone rang again.

*Unknown.*

I knew it was Leslie again, disguising her number. I still did not answer.

I poured another cup of coffee, put on a pair of sweatpants, and walked outside to get the paper.

The cool winter air hit my face as soon as I opened the door. I looked around the neighborhood as I walked to the end of the driveway to get the paper. With the exception of some people working on a house down the street, it was quiet as usual.

I could not help but think about how much I loved this neighborhood. It was where my life took shape. It was the place where wonderful memories developed, although they now seemed like distant dreams. It was this neighborhood, this village, where everyone took care of each other.

"This is better," I said softly to myself, thinking about Leslie's comment to me about deserving better.

When I returned to my porch, I heard a car pull into the driveway. I looked back and saw the black Mercedes. It was Leslie.

"Damn," I said as she emerged from her car.

I walked in the house, leaving the door open. I went into my bedroom to retrieve my cup of coffee. When I returned to the living room, the front door was closed and Leslie was sitting on the couch. I took a seat in the chair closer to the door, sipping my coffee and not saying a word.

"Smells like smoke in here," she said.

"I've been smoking," I responded drily.

"Thought you quit."

"And I thought we had this same conversation the other day," I said.

"Can I have some coffee?" she asked after a long and hard stare.

"You know where everything is. Go get it," I said blankly.

A few minutes later she returned from the kitchen and sat down quietly. I picked up the remote for the TV and hit the power button. The first thing that flashed across the screen was a commercial for *An Afternoon With Simone Jackson.*

Leslie and I watched the commercial and I began to stare hard at Simone. I started thinking again about her attractive features, but her eyes, for some reason, stood out above anything else. They seemed inviting to me. I saw something in her eyes in that brief thirty-second commercial that in the past five years I never saw in Leslie's eyes.

"I have tickets for her show on Thursday," Leslie said, breaking me out of my trance. I did not say a word.

I finished what was left in my cup and turned off the TV. I stood, reaching for the remote to the stereo, and hit play.

As the CD began to play, I grabbed the last cigarette out of the pack, sat back down, and lit it.

When the smooth piano riffs blared through the speakers, I closed my eyes and enjoyed the mellow sound. Leslie was talking, but I did not hear her. I heard nothing but the sound of a piano player playing an instrument as if he were the only one that could create the sweet, melodic tones. The music soothed me. It relaxed me. It gave me comfort. It gave me much-needed and desired peace.

After several moments, I opened my eyes. Leslie was no longer on the couch. Suddenly, she appeared at the entrance of the living room completely naked, wearing only a wicked smile. I stared at her beautiful, flawless bronze body, my southern territory begging me to let her invade, but my mind informed me that she was still the enemy.

When I stood up, she took that as a cue to return to my room. By the time I walked in, she had already stretched out on the bed. I picked her clothes up off the floor, then threw them toward her.

"I'm about to take a shower," I said.

She stared at me but did not move. Her face held a look of disbelief. I was no longer eager to step into her trap, and after realizing that, she climbed from the bed and put her bra and panties back on.

"You are really making this hard for me, aren't you?" she said as she dressed. "Do you not love me anymore?"

"I have a busy day, and I really need to take a shower so I can get it started," I said, avoiding answering the question.

Leslie finished dressing and grabbed her pocketbook. She stared at me, her brown eyes piercing my skin.

"I don't even know why I bother," she said, walking toward the front door and putting on her gloves. When she reached the door she paused.

"I am leaving for real this time." Her eyes pleaded. "I am not happy with Thomas. I want us to be together, Devlin."

I thought long before responding. My heart wanted to give in, but my brain was telling me the truth.

"I love you, Leslie," I said sincerely. "But the love I have for you has hurt me time and time again, and I refuse to continue to hurt." I paused and felt a strong pang run through my heart. "I'm sorry you're not happy in your marriage, but you chose to be there, just as I am choosing not to continue whatever this is we have."

She walked out of the house, leaving the door open. I closed the door behind her, walked back to my room, and sat on the bed.

As I sat there feeling sad, I heard Grammy talking to me again. Something she said to me years ago replayed in my mind.

"Baby, we live to learn so that we can learn to live."

* * *

After my shower, I decided to treat myself to a late lunch at one of my favorite restaurants, Backyard Grillin'. It was about a forty-five-minute drive from my house and I needed the ride to help clear my thoughts.

As the host guided me toward the bar, I looked around and saw couples and families dining together. I began to wonder if this was a good idea. Seeing all the happy faces, I became depressed.

"Sir, would you like a table once one becomes available?" the hostess asked.

I stared at her for a moment before answering no and taking a seat at the bar. After ordering a beer, I looked around the restaurant again, and it seemed as if the happy faces got happier as my sad heart became sadder.

I ordered the grilled shrimp and fish combo and I directed my eyes toward the TV that sat above the bar, trying to drown out all of the sounds of happiness surrounding me. I had made a huge mistake in choosing to have dinner when I was one miserable individual surrounded by happy couples and happy families.

After deciding to inform the server that I would like my dinner to go, I suddenly felt a light tap on my shoulder. When I turned around, I met eyes with a lovely woman. I felt my body melt.

"Devlin Carter?" she asked as she reached her hand out for me to shake.

"Yes," I replied, accepting her hand.

"Simone Jackson," she replied.

# 8

## *Simone*

After Tuesday's show, Charlene and I decided to have a late lunch at one of my favorite restaurants, Backyard Grillin'.

Once we arrived, it was unusually crowded for so late in the afternoon. The host seated us at a booth in the back near the bar. While sitting in our booth, I admired Charlene's zeal for her job and her youth. She was very wise and mature to be twenty-five. After we both ordered tea with lemon and began to scan the menu, I happened to look up and spotted him—Devlin Carter, the man who had been running through my mind for the past two days.

He was more handsome than the picture, and I could not take my eyes off him. I watched him as he took his brown leather jacket off and placed it on the chair beside him. He removed his glasses from his face after reading the menu and placed them in the case. I noticed the way he held his beer as he drank it. He licked his lips and my lady began to tingle at the sight. I was really beginning to feel ridiculous.

Charlene was talking, but I couldn't pay her any attention. My entire focus was on a man on the other side of the room.

"He's handsome," Charlene said, breaking me out of my trance.

"Who's handsome?" I asked, trying to hide my embarrassment.

"The man sitting at the bar that you've been staring at for the last few minutes," she said, smiling.

I was silent, wondering if I should tell her about the thoughts in my head. Something about Charlene made me feel comfortable about talking to her, so I told her who he was and the thoughts I had been having about him the past few days. I felt like we were all in high school and I was telling my best friend about a crush I had on the new boy in school.

"Go over and invite him to eat with us," she said.

I looked over at him, then turned back to Charlene.

"I can't do that. I've never approached a man in my life."

From the look on her face, I knew she did not believe me.

"Well, would you like me to go pass him a note?" she asked, laughing.

"No, I don't want you to pass him a note," I responded with a nervous and embarrassed laugh.

"Well, since he is going to be on the show Thursday, this is a good way to get the feel of him before then. Am I right?"

"Right," I said softly as I somehow got the courage to emerge from our booth and walk toward him.

The walk to the bar could not have been over eight feet, but it seemed like a mile. My heart began to pound furiously and I wanted to turn back, but my feet did not listen to my brain.

Once I reached him, he was looking up at the TV above the bar. I tapped him on his shoulder and he immediately turned around and looked directly into my eyes. Those hazel eyes were more hypnotic in person than on his picture.

"Devlin Carter?" I asked as I reached my hand out to him.

"Yes," he replied as he extended his hand.

"Simone Jackson," I said as I felt a strong surge run through my body from his touch.

"It's a pleasure to meet you," he said, smiling, making me feel all gushy inside.

There was a long silence and I felt nervous as all hell. I felt like a nutcase, standing there mute, not knowing what I should say next.

"Would you like to have a seat?" he asked, moving his jacket from the seat beside him and breaking our awkward silence.

"Umm," was all that seemed to come out. I was beginning to feel that I had made a mistake by approaching him, but I took a deep breath and tried again. "I was having lunch with my publicist when I noticed you sitting alone, and I thought I would ask if you would like to join us," I said as I began to feel a little more relaxed and easy when I saw him smile.

"I would love to join you," he responded quickly as he grabbed his jacket. After he instructed the bartender to have the server deliver his food to our booth, he followed me to our table.

Charlene slid over for me to sit beside her. Devlin sat directly in front of me.

After introducing Charlene to Devlin, there was more silence again. I did not know what to say, and he appeared to be at a loss for words as well.

I could feel Charlene staring at me, and then I felt her foot tap mine under the table, signaling me to say something.

"So are you ready for the show on Thursday?" I asked,

immediately thinking how dumb that question was. I was beginning to feel embarrassed again. I could not believe that despite all the interviews I had done in my life, I finally met someone who intimidated me for reasons beyond my understanding.

He looked at me with those soothing hazel marbles again and I felt my entire body go numb. I could not think of a time that I had ever felt this way about a man or a woman. As strange as it was, this feeling had to have also been the most wonderful feeling that I had ever experienced in my life—a feeling I wanted to welcome with open arms.

"As a matter of fact, I am very excited about being on your show," he said, sipping his beer. Again, we all became silent.

I could feel Charlene's eyes pierce my side as if she were trying to tell me something, but I did my best to ignore her.

"Mr. Carter," Charlene started, breaking the silence. "Who's your publicist?"

He turned his eyes away from me and looked over to her. With his eyes no longer on me, it felt as if a cloud had covered the sun.

"Please call me Devlin," he began. "My business manager has actually been handling most of my engagements," he said to her as I continued to watch him.

Once the server brought his meal to him, I realized that Charlene and I had not ordered yet.

When we placed our order, he moved his plate over to the side and told us that he would wait for us. He appeared to be exactly what I imagined him to be, a true Southern gentleman.

Shortly after we finished eating, Charlene announced that it was time for her to go, leaving Devlin and me alone.

The three of us had sat in the booth for what seemed like hours, so by the time she left, I was no longer nervous and had really come to enjoy his eyes on me.

I still felt weird because I still couldn't grasp what made me so attracted to this man prior to actually meeting him, but as we sat at the table alone and talked, I began to see the person behind the picture and promotional information. Everything that I had imagined over the past few days about him was true.

We sat alone in the booth until about seven PM talking and enjoying each other's company tremendously. Both of our phones rang at different times throughout the evening, but we did not bother to answer them. It appeared that the only thing either one of us cared to focus on was each other.

As we walked out of the restaurant together, one of the servers asked for my autograph.

"Ms. Jackson, I just want you to know that I watch your show every day and when I can't, I make sure I tape it," she said to me as I signed her napkin.

"You must really love the attention," Devlin said as we walked out of the door together.

After he walked me to my car, we stared into each other's eyes, and I felt something that made my heart dance. I thought about the comment he made a few moments earlier about loving the attention. I did love attention, but the attention I had received from him in those few short hours was more special to me than any attention I had received during all my years in the business.

After getting into my car, I looked at the LCD screen on my phone. I had six missed calls and four messages.

"Where are you, love?" the Jamaican accent asked on the first message. "I've been trying to call you for the past hour. Call me soon."

The other three messages were also from Trinity, so I did not bother to listen.

When I pulled into my driveway, my phone rang again. I initially thought it was Trinity again, but the ID displayed a local number I did not recognize.

"Hello?" I asked cautiously. Not many people had this number.

"Simone, it's me, Charlene."

"Hey," I said, relieved that it was someone I recognized.

"I've been thinking since I left you guys earlier." She paused. "Since it's evident that you would like to get to know Devlin, and I can tell from the look in his eyes he would like to get to know you too, I think it would be a good idea to put you guys together as something like a couple. Have you go to events together and whatnot. Both of you are successful and very well known. It's almost like a match made in heaven," she said, giggling.

I did not respond, but I felt a huge smile form on my face as I entered my front door. I told her I would think about it, and danced a little love dance all the way to my bathroom to begin my bathwater. I could still smell his cologne from when he hugged me as we said our good-byes. The smell was so sweet, so seductive. I began to feel that tingle again.

My thoughts were so engrossed with Devlin that I had totally forgotten about calling Trinity back.

I lay in my tub with my eyes closed, imagining him inside the warm water, caressing my entire body. I rubbed my left nipple with my right hand, and moved my left hand down to my southern territory and began to rub my lady. I felt more pleasure in pleasing myself while wishing it was Devlin than I had felt with anyone in my life.

My lady began to jump with pure excitement, and my body followed her. As I squirmed around in the warm water, I felt myself begin to explode with utmost pleasure.

I yelled out loud without control. Passion stormed my body as if it were a hurricane on the coast of Florida.

*Ring, ring.*

"Shit!" I yelled aloud. I looked at the ID.

*Trinity.*

"Yes?" I asked drily.

"Love, where have you been? I have been trying to call you all day. I was beginning to get worried," she said.

"Everything's fine, Trinity. Had a long day and just got in."

There was a long silence between the two of us.

"Are you sure, love?" she asked.

"More than positive," I responded drily again, pissed as hell at her timing.

"I have some bad news. I will not be able to make it this weekend. I recently obtained a new client. One of those little one-hit wonder singers, and I will be on set with her shooting her new video this weekend." She paused as if she was waiting for me to respond. I said nothing.

"Are you there, love?" she asked.

"Trinity, that is more than fine. Look, I am in the tub and I am exhausted. Call me tomorrow, okay?"

There was another long pause.

"Are you angry, love?" she asked.

*Yes, I'm angry. You just fucked up my nut, heifer,* I thought.

"No, Trinity, I'm not angry at all, just tired. Call me tomorrow, okay?" I hung up without waiting for her to respond.

After getting out of the tub, I moved my little party to my bedroom, where I finished what Trinity had interrupted. It was not the hurricane explosion that I was about to have before Trinity interrupted, but it was enough to verify that I desired this man.

After my moment of self-fornication, I felt weird. I had

pleased myself several times over the years, but this was the first time that I had seriously thought of someone while doing it.

I began to wonder if Devlin Carter could make me explode in person just as he had done by merely being in my thoughts.

"My Darius Lovehall?" I wondered.

# 9

# *Devlin*

On my way home from the restaurant, I felt as if I had been renewed. It was almost as if new breath had emerged from nowhere to give me hope of better days.

I was initially shocked when Simone came over to introduce herself to me, but I was very stunned when she invited me to have dinner with her.

As I sat at the table, I found myself totally immersed in her. I did not want to take my eyes off her beauty. She was far more attractive in person than I imagined she would be, and while sitting there with her, I could not stop imagining what it would be like to spend time with her.

As I drove home, all my thoughts were on Simone Jackson. When we first shook hands, feelings that were new to me began to emerge in my mind. She must have had the same feelings, because it appeared that she watched my every move too. But I learned a long time ago that a look from a woman did not always mean that she was attracted to you.

After her publicist left, I assumed that Simone was

going to leave as well, but we remained in the booth talking about almost everything under the sun. She asked me questions about my products and my family, and I felt incredibly comfortable with revealing things to her. It truly amazed me that I felt more trust from her in a few hours than I had felt for Leslie in five years.

I pulled into my driveway feeling like I was on cloud nine and nothing could knock me down.

A sudden strange and cold feeling came over me when I walked into my house. As I placed my phone on the charger, I remembered that it had rung several times while at the restaurant, but I never answered. I had assumed that it was Leslie and did not want to be bothered with her foolishness while enjoying the company of a beautiful and intelligent woman.

I looked at the LCD screen and noticed I had eight missed calls. When I reviewed the missed calls and noticed the name that came up all eight times, my heart fell as if it had dropped down to my feet.

*Stephanie's cell.*

My hands trembled as I pressed the buttons to listen to my messages.

"Devlin, Jacob went into a coma." She paused and I could tell that she was trying to hold back her tears. "We're at Carolina Medical Center. I'm sorry if I am disturbing you, but I just thought that you would like to know."

I sat down on the couch when a sudden and strong feeling of guilt showered my body. Ms. Betty's words from the other day came to mind.

"Living ain't easy, chile, and it's even harder when those you love go on to meet the Lawd. You be strong, you hear me? You spend as much time with that boy while he still be here."

I felt guilty for having a good evening while my friend's life appeared to be ending.

Tears fell uncontrollably from my eyes. I tried calling Stephanie back, but all I got was her voice mail.

I needed to talk to someone, but I had no one to call. God had stolen everyone from me.

"Damn you, God!" I yelled. I was angry. I was hurting, and there was no one there to comfort me.

I grabbed my jacket and walked out of the house to my car, still cursing God, asking Him why He chose me for this pain.

"What have I done so bad, God?" I asked as I sat in my car. "Why are you taking everyone from me?"

While I drove, I got a sudden urge to call Simone. Right before we left the restaurant, we exchanged numbers. I had not planned to call her so soon, but for some reason, I felt a need to speak to her.

"Hello?" the sleepy voice answered.

"Simone?" I asked and then paused, feeling that I made a mistake in calling her. This woman and I had just met and here I was calling her as if we had known each other all of our lives. "This is Devlin. Did I wake you?" I immediately felt dumb for asking an obvious question. I could tell from her voice that she had been asleep.

"Hey," she responded as if she made a sudden transition from asleep to awake.

There was a long silence and I couldn't talk. Why did I call her?

"I'm sorry for calling," I uttered. "But something just came up and I didn't know who else to call, and for some reason, I chose you."

There was more silence. I could hear her shifting in her bed as if she was getting up.

"What's wrong?" she asked.

I really felt stupid. I called a complete stranger during my time of need and could not even talk to her about what was going on.

"My best friend went into a coma tonight while you and I were out earlier. His wife tried calling me and I didn't get the message until I arrived home." I paused, taking a breath, trying not to break down. "I'm headed to the hospital now and for some reason, I called you. I can't really explain why, but there was something about you that made me feel comfortable."

"Devlin," she began. "For whatever this is worth, I'm glad that you felt comfortable in calling me. Is there anything I can do?"

"Just hearing that was enough," I said solemnly.

"What hospital is he at?" she asked me.

"He's at Carolina Medical Center." I paused again, really feeling awkward. "Look, I apologize for waking you up. Thanks a million for accepting my call." Then I hung up without saying bye.

When I arrived at the hospital, Jacob's brother, Trevor, was sitting in the downstairs lobby alone. He looked high and I was sure he was.

"Where's everybody?" I asked.

When he looked up at me, he burst out into a loud cry. I hated to think it, but I wondered if his crying was because of his brother's ailing health, or the fact that he would no longer have his own personal bank.

Trevor was Jacob's older brother who dropped out of college his sophomore year because he was not getting the playing time he thought he deserved on the football team. Since then he never really had a job and pretty much lived off the success of Jacob.

"Devlin, why did it have to be him, man?" he asked me. "I should be the one dying, not Jacob, man. Not Jacob."

I took a seat on the bench beside him, his sincere tears answering any doubt I had. I always knew that he really loved Jacob; we all did. We all felt the pain that Jacob had gone through.

I sat with Trevor for about fifteen minutes, trying to console him, trying to help him make sense of a situation I did not even understand. I felt like the blind leading the blind. I could not think of any consoling words for him; I had none for me. I knew how Trevor was feeling. I grew up with both of them. They were family; they were the closest things to brothers I had ever known. I felt the same pain of losing a brother as Trevor.

Trevor told me that the rest of the family was in the waiting room on the fourth floor. I tried to talk him into going up with me, but he declined.

I walked to the elevator and hit the up button when I heard someone calling my name. When I looked back to see who was calling me, I was shocked, yet—at the same time—very pleased. It was Simone.

Her hair was pulled back into a bun and she looked very different from the way she wore it earlier. She wrapped her brown leather jacket tightly around her waist and her blue jeans covered her brown suede boots. She did not have on any makeup, which, to me, made her look more stunning than she did earlier.

"What are you doing here?" I asked as she opened her arms to hug me.

"I heard a friend needed a friend," she said as she looked directly into my eyes.

When we arrived at the waiting room on the fourth floor, the entire room was packed. Not only with Jacob's family, but other families who also had loved ones in their last hours.

I began looking around for familiar faces when I saw Cody's head resting in the lap of Jacob's mother. When she spotted Simone and me, she waved us over.

"Hey, Devlin," she said as she woke Cody so that she could move to give me a hug. After we embraced, I introduced her to Simone.

"Mrs. Brown, I remember meeting you a few years ago when Jacob was on my show," Simone said to her as she gave her a hug as well.

I had totally forgotten that Jacob told me about the interview with her, but I was even more impressed that Simone remembered.

*Maybe she was the right person to call*, I thought.

After sitting back down, she told me that Stephanie, Li'l J, and Mr. Brown were in the room with Jacob and that I could go see him after their visit.

When I asked Mrs. Brown what happened, her smile weakened. She looked at me with tired eyes.

"Something told me this morning when I got up to go see my baby boy." She paused and dabbed her eyes with a white handkerchief. "And while I was sitting there with him, he just drifted away."

I should have been there. If my friend was leaving, I wanted to say good-bye. I had to say good-bye. I needed to say good-bye. I began to get angry with God again. He stole from me the opportunity to tell Grammy good-bye and it looked like He was stealing my chance to tell Jacob good-bye as well.

As we sat in the waiting room, Mrs. Brown and Simone began having small conversations about nothing. I do not know exactly when it happened, but after several moments, I realized that Simone was holding my hand. Suddenly the weight I had been carrying did not seem so heavy.

I was deep into my thoughts when I looked up and saw Trevor walk through the doors of the waiting room. I do not think his mother was even aware that he had been down in the lobby because when she saw him, she quickly emerged from her seat and ran to her oldest son.

"Praise God! Praise God!" she yelled as she ran toward Trevor and hugged him. It was a touching moment, and I noticed that it had even brought a tear to Simone's eyes.

I introduced Simone to Trevor and he took a seat beside me.

"Glad you decided to come up," I said as I reached my free hand to him to shake.

Cody came over to him, climbed on his lap, and went back to sleep.

It was almost an hour before Mr. Brown and Li'l J returned to the waiting room and by that time, Simone had made herself comfortable by laying her head on my shoulder. The way we had interacted the entire day, at the restaurant and here at the hospital, someone could have mistaken us as a couple.

It was time for Trevor and me to take what could be our last visit with Jacob. I was nervous about how I would act to see my best friend in this state, but I wanted to say bye.

As I emerged from the chair I was sitting in, I felt nervous. I was afraid. I did not know what to expect when I saw him. I looked over at Simone before walking out of the waiting room, and looking into her eyes gave me the strength I needed.

When Trevor and I walked into the room together, we noticed Stephanie sitting in a chair beside Jacob, holding his hand. When she saw us both come in, she walked over and the three of us had a group hug. She then returned to the chair and stared at her husband through rivers of tears.

Trevor could not control himself. Although I wanted to break down, I knew someone had to be strong, or at least pretend to be. We all remained in the room just watching Jacob lay with his eyes closed and breathing faintly. I looked at the mighty warrior stripped of his life so early.

Who would look after his family? Who would look after me? Those two questions ran through my mind the entire time, but answers refused to come.

After sitting in the room for about thirty minutes, I left Trevor and Stephanie in the room with Jacob and returned to the waiting room. I sat back down in the chair beside Simone and she immediately grabbed my hand again. It warmed my cold heart. It warmed my cold soul.

Around one in the morning, my eyes suddenly opened. We had all drifted off, and Simone lay wrapped in my arms with her head lying on my chest, which brought a moment of peace.

Her sudden friendship warmed me tremendously. Earlier I was feeling guilty for having dinner with her instead of being with Jacob, but maybe God directed us to meet earlier for a reason. Maybe God knew that I needed someone new in my life. Maybe God did remember me after all.

I was thinking about that day, the good and the bad, and everyone jumped when we heard a loud yell come from the hallway.

"Noooooo, noooooooo!" It was Trevor informing the world that my friend, our brother, was gone.

# 10

## *Simone*

I was sitting in my office behind my desk at six-forty AM, thinking about the past eight and a half hours of my life. One minute I was in my bed asleep, the next I found myself driving to the hospital to console a man I had just met.

When Devlin called me, I could hear the hurt in his voice about his friend Jacob. Even though he did not say it, I could tell that he was feeling guilty for not answering his phone earlier while we were together.

As I drove to the Carolina Medical Center, I wondered if I was overstepping boundaries. I did not want him to feel as if I was pushing my kindness or myself on him, but I could tell he was hurting and I remembered him telling me at dinner how alone he felt in the world.

When I walked into the lobby of the hospital and saw him at the elevator, I was nervous about how he would react to seeing me. I called his name and walked toward him. We immediately embraced. Once we let go, I saw the hurt and the pain in his eyes, and I wished that there was something I could have done to stop it.

I had never been in a situation like that, so I really did not know what to say. I could remember as a child my dad always seemed to know the exact words to say to those in bereavement, but for me, I always felt as if I would say the wrong thing.

While we sat in the waiting room, I reached for his hand to hold. The feeling was warm; not a sexual warmth, but almost as if there was a connection between the two of us. Our connection made me feel what he was feeling. When he came back into the waiting room from visiting with Jacob, the look on his face made me feel the pain he was feeling. Once he sat back down, I grabbed his hand again as I had earlier. I lay my head on his chest. The next thing I remembered was waking up after hearing the cries from Trevor when Jacob passed around one AM.

Jacob's family appeared to be strong, with the exception of his brother. I was amazed at the poise of his two sons. They were deeply hurt, but it was obvious that they were prepared for this day.

Devlin and I left the hospital together around two and decided to go to a nearby Waffle House to have breakfast. It had been so long since I had been up that late, and I was surprised that I was not sleepy.

We sat in our booth and were very quiet. I really did not know what to say and was afraid that I might say something wrong, so I allowed him time to grieve and talk when he was ready. I learned as a talk-show host to allow people to speak when they felt the time to, and not to pry too hard.

"Twenty-four years," he whispered. I remained silent.

"He was the only true friend I ever had. I was the best man at his wedding, and he was supposed to be the best man at mine," he said, followed by more silence.

I felt my eyes begin to water again, not only for his loss, but for the realization that I had never been that close with anyone in my life. Even with people I was involved with, I do not think I shared a bond the way that Devlin and Jacob had.

Sitting there with him, I realized that although Devlin and I experienced life somewhat differently, we both experienced the same hopes and wishes.

He took a sip of his coffee and looked up at me.

"Thanks," he said.

"For what?" I asked.

"For coming tonight. When I called you earlier, it was done out of desperation. I didn't know anyone else I could call."

Again, more silence.

"I . . ." He paused and took another sip of his coffee. "I have been in a relationship with an involved woman for over five years."

For some reason, that revelation surprised me, and I really did not know where he was going or even how to respond.

"I know you're wondering why I'm telling you this," he said.

I slowly nodded my head.

"This past Sunday, I went to see Jacob. That was the last time we talked." He paused again and I saw tears fall from those hazel eyes. "For the past few weeks, I had been trying to end the relationship, but seemed to always find myself right back in, not letting go, realizing that I was not even putting an effort in letting go."

More silence. I did not say a word. I just listened.

"When I got home on Sunday evening, she was at my house waiting for me in my driveway. She asked where I had been, and when I told her, the next thing out of her mouth was criticism about the house I live in and the car I drive. Not once did she ask about Jacob."

He reached for a napkin to wipe his face.

"I ended it then. She's called and has come by the past couple of days, but I no longer entertain the thought of us being together."

I wanted to say something, but I was honestly at a loss for words. I understood him. I heard what he said without him saying the obvious.

"Tonight when I got the message from Stephanie, it never crossed my mind to call her. Actually, she had not crossed my mind since I met you until now. For some strange reason, I felt more inclined to call you than her."

He paused again and suddenly I felt the tears fall from my eyes.

"I'm glad you called," I whispered.

I did not get home until around four. I immediately jumped into the shower and got ready to go to the studio. On my drive there, I thought about the openness Devlin had with me. I thought about his honesty. Although most of our time spent was due to a tragic moment in his life, I knew that he was genuine.

I also thought about his openness about his recent relationship. Then I thought about my own. Could I tell him? Would he understand me the way I did him?

"Good morning, crumb cake," Suzette said, breaking me from my trance, standing at the entrance to my office.

"Hey, Suze, how are you this morning?" I said half-dry, half-enthusiastic.

"Honey, you look like you pulled an all-nighter. I need to get makeup and hair in here an hour earlier than usual." She paused to chuckle. "Is everything all right?"

I went on to explain to Suzette the last few hours of my day, and when I was done, she had the hugest smile on her face.

"Why are you smiling?" I asked, a little pissed at what I thought was insensitivity.

She walked into my office and took a seat in the chair in front of my desk.

"It's been what, two days since our last real conversation?" she started.

I was not quite sure where she was coming from.

"So, has the estranged daughter finally found her Damien Lovehall?"

That statement brought a huge smile to my weary face.

"It's Darius Lovehall, Suzette," I responded.

After the morning taping, I called Devlin, but all I got was his voice mail. As soon as I hung up the phone after leaving a message, it rang. I thought it was him and did not bother to look at the caller ID when I answered.

"Hey, Devlin, how are you feeling this morning?"

"Who's Devlin?" Trinity asked.

*Shit*, I thought. I really did not want to have this type of conversation with Trinity, although I had the feeling that soon it would be coming.

"He's a future guest of the show."

"Why would he call your cell, love?" she asked.

I paused for a few moments, thinking about what I was going to say, and before I knew it, my mouth was moving.

"Trinity, as I'm sure you know, for a while I haven't been happy with my life. I haven't been happy with us. Yes, as I stated earlier, Devlin is a future guest, but he's also someone I think I would like to get to know." I paused to hear if she would have a response, but all I heard was breathing.

"Trinity, are you there?" I asked right before she hung up.

A few moments later, my phone rang again, but this time I was sure to look at the calling number before answering.

*Devlin.*

"Hey," I said, happy to hear his voice, quickly forgetting about Trinity.

"Sorry I missed your call earlier. I just woke up and got out of the shower."

"It's no problem. I was just calling to say hello and to see how you were feeling this morning," I said.

There was a long silence, and it was beginning to make me feel a little awkward.

"I want to apologize for keeping you up all night and boring you with my life story."

"Devlin, you did not bore me, and I was glad to know that I am someone you felt who you could confide in," I said, smiling.

He started to laugh softly. I wondered what it was that he found funny and hoped that he would share it with me.

"You know, I can see how you got your job. Either you are an excellent bullshitter, or you are the genuine article. You are a great listener, and I just wanted to thank you, as well as apologize for last night."

I really began to cheese all up after that comment. I felt like a little schoolgirl.

"Mr. Carter, I can tell you that I am all one-hundred percent grade A bullshit," I said and we both laughed.

We remained on the phone for about thirty more minutes, and it was honestly the best conversation I'd had with anyone in a very long time.

After hanging up with Devlin, I walked over to Suzette's office to inform her that we would have to cancel Devlin's segment on Thursday's show. I also told her that I wanted to cancel Monday's taping so that I could attend the funeral with Devlin.

I left the studio around two PM and on my way home, all I could do was think of Devlin. I was becoming more and more intrigued about this man. I could see and feel his passion. I could see and feel his honesty. I knew he was the genuine article from the first time I saw his picture and read his bio.

Once I got home, I headed straight for my bedroom and to my bed. I was sleepy as hell, but Devlin stayed on my mind. I thought about how I felt thinking of him in the tub. I thought about the dinner we shared and how I felt comfortable at the hospital when I nestled my head in his chest.

After turning the ringers off on all the phones in my house so that I would not be disturbed, I climbed into my bed and grabbed the huge pillow that lay across the headboard. I cuddled with it, wishing it were Devlin, hoping that he would soon be my Darius Lovehall.

# 11
## *Devlin*

It was five o'clock in the morning when I got back home and as tired as I was, I couldn't sleep. My eyes refused to close. I stared at the dark ceiling, thinking about Jacob, remembering the times we spent together as kids. I thought about the time that Grammy spanked us both because we stole candy from the store on the corner.

"Y'all boys know betteren that," she had said. "Devlin, you know what to do."

And I did. I had to go out to the weeping willow tree in the backyard and retrieve four of its branches. When I returned to the house with the four branches, I handed them to Grammy and she began to braid them together.

"Y'all boys know good as day stealing is wrong," she had muttered as she finished the last braid. "And if you don't know, you's 'bout to learn now."

She whipped Jacob and me until she got tired.

I eventually drifted off to sleep, thinking about the love I had for them and the love they had for me. I woke up later that morning but continued to lie in the bed thinking about everyone who had come and gone in my life. I also thought about the strange dreams I had.

I could not understand the dream. I had stood near the bank of a pond. I suddenly fell in. I was drowning, but before I went completely under, flashes of Grammy, Jacob, and other people I didn't know sprang to mind.

Sadness invaded my body and my mind. I knew this day was coming, and Jacob did his best to help prepare us all, but there was never a way to prepare for death.

I threw on a pair of sweats, slipped on my slippers, and went to get the paper. As soon as I picked it up, the headline yelled at me.

*LOCAL FOOTBALL STAR, DEAD AT 32.*

The headline brought tears to my eyes. I slowly went back into the house, threw the paper on the coffee table, and headed straight to the bathroom for a long and hot shower.

The water poured down my face, mingling with my continuous flow of tears. I began to question God again when I suddenly thought about Simone.

Why had I been so honest with her earlier that morning? It was her sincerity when she showed up at the hospital. She seemed so concerned that I was hurting inside. And she was beautiful. During our time together, I discovered that she was not only beautiful on the outside, but there was also beauty within.

How had a woman that I had just met become someone I could confide in so quickly? I did not feel less than a man when I cried around her, and I was not embarrassed. The way she held my hand to comfort me was pure and said a lot about her.

I heard a sudden whisper that I could not quite understand, but it eased my pain. I climbed out of the shower and heard my phone beep. I had a missed call.

*Simone.*

I smiled and immediately returned the call. Talking to her was easy. I could never talk with Leslie this way. Leslie's conversations were about how unhappy she was and her mistake in marrying Thomas. Any time I discussed me, she rarely listened or showed any concern. It was always all about her.

After hanging up the phone with Simone, I began to feel better. She was more understanding than any woman I had ever known

I decided to go to Jacob's house to be with what was left of my extended family. Once I arrived, there were dozens of people standing on the lawn. Some were reporters; others came to show their final respects to a local star athlete.

I parked my car about a block from the house and called to let Stephanie know I was there. When I entered the house, I saw faces I had not seen in years. Some were friends I had not seen since high school. Some were Jacob and Stephanie's family members that I had not seen since their wedding.

After speaking to several people, I walked upstairs to Jacob's hideaway room. I wanted to get away from everyone else for a few moments and sit in the room where he had spent most of the end of his life.

The room was dark and the shades on both windows were down. I walked over to the window that faced the front yard and pulled up the shade. As I turned to walk to the next window, I noticed Li'l J sitting on the couch. He startled me.

"What's up, Uncle Dev?" he asked sadly.

"Not much, J. Just trying to maintain," I said.

After letting the shade up on the second window, I walked back over to the couch and took a seat on the other side.

We sat in silence, the voices from downstairs drifting into the room.

"I miss him already," he finally said.

He held a large manila envelope on his lap. I knew what it was. Jacob told me about it months ago. Li'l J saw that I noticed.

"I'm scared to open it," he whispered.

"Don't be."

"Why did he have to go now?" he asked, but I had no answer.

Approximately thirty minutes had passed when Li'l J started to open the package. I took that as my cue to leave him alone.

As I closed the door behind me, I noticed Stephanie standing at the top of the steps with another envelope in her arms.

I could tell she had not slept. Her eyes were heavy and full of grief. We embraced and remained that way for several minutes. She asked me to join her in their bedroom. The room was huge, with a balcony overlooking the pool in the backyard.

"I need a cigarette," she said.

"I thought you quit," I reminded her.

"I thought you did too," she said with a weary smile. "I smell it on you."

I smiled and pulled out the pack that was inside my jacket pocket. We stepped onto the balcony and silently puffed the white sticks, hoping the deadly smoke would help us to find a moment of peace, a moment of refuge. We both started smoking years ago, thinking that it would be a refuge from the pain. She was coping with the news of Jacob's illness that would eventually take her husband and disrupt their life; I was dealing with the sudden death of my grandmother.

As we looked out over the pool and into the spacious backyard, I noticed that she still held onto the envelope.

Jacob had made videos for his wife and two boys. He said that he wanted to leave something for them to have that was directly from him to them in conversation form.

"Are you and Simone Jackson a couple now?" she asked.

"No." I paused to inhale and slowly exhale. "As a matter of fact, we met for the first time yesterday afternoon at Backyard Grillin'."

I saw a weak smile come across her face.

"Jacob was right, then."

"What do you mean?" I asked.

She took another pull from her cigarette. She handed me the package she had been holding.

I immediately read the label. *Mr. Devlin Lamont Carter*. I smiled when I saw my full name.

"Let's go back downstairs," she said.

I remained at the house until around eight PM then I drove home in silence and thought about my friend. I wondered if he and Grammy had found each other in heaven yet. Would I ever make it there myself to see both of them again?

The first thing I did at home was open the package. It contained a smaller yellow envelope and a DVD. The smaller envelope had a small key inside. I placed the key on the coffee table and placed the DVD into the player.

Immediately after I hit the play button, Jacob's smiling face appeared on the screen.

"What's up, black man?" he began.

My eyes filled with tears.

"Well, if you are looking at this, you already know where I am." He chuckled a little. "I told you a few months ago that I was making a video for the family, so receiving one too should not have come as a big surprise." He paused and took a drink of water. "Since we were eight, there hasn't been a moment in either of our lives that we didn't share. Our first dates when we were fifteen. Remember the twins?" he asked as he began laughing.

I laughed and wiped my tears as I continued to listen to my friend.

"We felt each other's pain. What I went through, you went through. What you went through, I went through." He paused again, and a look of seriousness formed on his face. "I never attempted to get in your business and tell you right from wrong. We were both raised to know the difference. But now in my death, I refuse to stay silent on the matter." He paused again and stared directly into the camera. He took another sip of his water, then spoke again.

"Leslie is drowning you. She has been drowning you for years. I never told you this and I have always felt guilty for sitting in silence, but my silence has come to an end now. You have always known that she could not make you happy. All she has done is make you content, and we both know that content does not equate to happy. I want the best for you, just as you have always wanted the best for me. You're now the dominant male figure in both my sons' lives, and I be damned if I am going to let their role model go down like a pussy." He laughed so hard after saying that, that he coughed uncontrollably.

"All I'm trying to say, man, is that I love you. I know that you feel that you are all alone now, but you are not. I will always be somewhere in you. You still have Stephanie and the boys as family. They are a part of me, and that makes them a part of you." He paused and suddenly tears began to fall from his eyes.

"There is someone out there that's going to be there for you, but there are two people holding you back from receiving her into your life. One of those persons is a pure heifer, no name needed, and you need to dismiss her. The other . . ." He paused. "The other, well, he has to die in order for her to come."

I quickly grabbed the remote to pause the video. My heart pounded profusely. I did not know what to think about Jacob's last comment.

Simone suddenly came across my mind. I thought about the day before. I told Leslie good-bye, then decided to go out to eat, where unexpectedly, I met Simone. Then I got the call from Stephanie informing me that Jacob went into a coma, and then Simone met me at the hospital.

More tears began to fall as I pushed the play button for Jacob to continue.

"My best friend is drowning, and I want to save him. I am at peace, brother. I know my family is well taken care of financially and spiritually, and I know you will be there to teach my boys how to be men."

Before the video stopped, I noticed the date and time. He had recorded this shortly after I had left his house that past Sunday. The TV screen became a blanket of fuzzy static. I did not bother to hit the stop button, just remained there, staring at the TV.

Suddenly, Jacob's face reappeared on the screen.

"I know you're wondering what the key is for, right?" He started laughing. "I almost forgot myself. One day soon, Trevor is going to have a talk with you. After the two of you talk, go to my house, and behind the picture of my family in my hideaway, there is a safe; the key opens the safe. Inside you will find a package there for him." He paused again. "Now, you may have a hundred conversations with him before you do this, but I promise you that you will know when it's time." The tape ended and I digested the last words I would ever hear from my brother.

I pulled my wallet out of my pocket and placed the key

in one of the compartments. I went to my room, lay across my bed, and grabbed my phone.

"Hello?" Simone said softly.

"Hey, are you asleep?" I asked, hoping I had not wakened her.

"No, I've been asleep most of the day. Now I'm just laying in my bed thinking about you."

That comment startled me. I smiled.

"Are you okay?" she asked.

"Believe it or not, I'm doing well," I said.

There was a long silence.

"Would you like to come over?" she asked.

Again I was shocked, but very pleased.

"I would love to come over. Give me a few moments to shower then I will call for directions, okay?"

# 12

## *Simone*

*What the hell did I just do?* I asked myself.

I could not believe that I had just invited Devlin over to my house. As soon as I hung up the phone, I jumped out of my bed and headed to the bathroom to take a quick shower.

While the water gently massaged my skin, my entire body trembled. The sexual thoughts I had about him, and the passion I lost myself in whenever I dreamed of him, returned.

I thought about the feeling that I received when we first shook hands and the conversations we shared. He was more than I had even imagined.

I dried off, thinking about all the books and movies I had read or seen where the main character met her soul mate and they lived happily ever after. I never thought that happened in real life, but now I was thinking that maybe I could have been wrong. Maybe it could happen for me.

I rushed into my room looking for something to wear. I had to make sure that I wore the right thing, but despite all the clothes I owned, I couldn't find anything that felt right.

I pulled out several things before deciding that I wanted to be comfortable and look casual. I threw on a pair of old jeans, one of my old AUM sweatshirts, and a camisole instead of a bra.

As I pulled my hair back into one big ponytail, my doorbell rang. I froze. My heart pounded like it was trying to break free from my chest.

"Get it together, Simone," I whispered to myself.

This man was inside my mind. Why? Why was I attracted to him? Why did I want to know more about him? Why did I invite him over to my house at eleven o'clock at night?

I looked through the peephole and saw a fine golden man standing outside of my door. My body switched from tremble mode to pure peace.

"What's going on?" Devlin asked as I opened the door and reached into him for a hug.

The embrace sent me back to trembling mode.

*Be cool, Simone, be cool,* I thought.

But I began to giggle like a little girl with a crazy crush. These feelings were new to me. It was something that I could grow to love.

He followed me through my huge hallway and up the stairs to my den. I invited him to have a seat on the couch in front of the TV and excused myself. In those few moments from the door to the den, my lady had become so moist that she was dripping.

I grabbed a towel out of the bathroom closet and ran warm water over it. After quickly wiping my lady, I returned to Devlin, who stood at my entertainment center observing my DVD collection.

"*Love Jones,*" he said, reaching for the case. "This is one of my favorites. Mind if we watch it?"

*Could he be my Darius Lovehall?* I asked myself.

I could not speak, stunned that he had chosen *Love Jones*. I just nodded my head and smiled.

Halfway through the movie, my head was on his lap. The feelings had gone beyond any feeling I had ever had in my life. He gave me a light neck massage and I felt like I was in heaven.

"So, do you give full body massages?" I asked seductively.

"Do you have any oils?" he responded.

I quickly jumped up from the couch and ran to my bathroom. I returned with a blanket, so that I could lie on the floor, and a bottle of wild cherry–scented body oil.

Devlin smiled at me. I pulled off my sweatshirt and dropped to the floor to lie on my stomach.

"Are you sure you're ready for this pleasure?" he asked with a seductive tone that turned me on.

"Yes," I whispered.

Devlin sat beside me. I closed my eyes and imagined what was about to happen.

"You know this will have to come off, right?" he asked, pointing to my camisole.

I sat up slowly, pulled the camisole over my head, and tossed it gently to his side. I hesitated a second, allowing his eyes to linger on my bare breasts. Then I slowly repositioned myself back on the blanket.

Cool oil suddenly dripped down my back, making me squirm.

"Sorry," Devlin said as he warmed the oil with his hands and gently rubbed my back.

My eyes were closed, but I dared not fall asleep. His touch was unlike any I had felt in my thirty-two years. His hands gave passion. My lady moistened again.

"That feels good," I moaned.

Devlin remained silent as he pleasured my body with

his gentle touch. My lady began to throb, although his hands never got close to her. I felt as if I were going to explode as I lay on the blanket.

"Are you okay?" he asked softly.

"Um-huh," I said, trying to hold in the things I really wanted to say.

"Do you want me to stop?" he asked.

"You better not," I whimpered softly. "It feels good."

His hands moved to my neck and hit a spot right above my shoulder that made every part of my body shake. A pulsing sensation spread throughout my body. If he was touching me, I could not feel it. It was an orgasm that mere words could not fully explain.

I did not want it to end. I did not want time to leave me.

"Are you sure you're okay?" he asked again. I responded by slowly shaking my head yes.

I lay on the floor, still basking in the moment of ecstasy.

"May I use your bathroom, please?" he asked.

"Sure, follow me."

He grabbed my hand as we walked through the dim hallway and reached the bathroom door. The tremble in my body began again. When we reached the bathroom, he kissed me like no man or woman had ever kissed me.

Devlin broke away from me and our eyes met.

"You're beautiful," he told me.

"You're handsome," I replied.

When he went into the bathroom, I quickly ran back to the bathroom in my bedroom to wipe myself again.

"You are acting foolish, Simone," I said aloud. "Calm your ass down."

I wanted Devlin to make love to me. I wanted to feel his passion completely, but I also wanted to wait. I did not want to rush and have him think that I was some kind of slut. I was nervous because I knew that if we continued to kiss, I would be putty in his hands.

When I returned to the den, Devlin was on the couch, putting on his shoes.

"You're not leaving, are you?" I asked, disappointed.

"Yes. I think that we may not be too pleased with ourselves in the morning if I didn't leave now."

I smiled sadly.

"You are definitely a true Southern gentleman," I said.

"That's what my grammy raised me to be. That's all I know how to be."

I wished he would stay and never leave. He awoke a part of me that had long been asleep, and I never wanted it to return to its slumber.

I reached for him, brought him into me, and kissed him gently.

Once we broke away, our eyes met again.

"Would you be my Darius Lovehall?" I whispered to him.

"Only if you would be my Nina Mosley," he responded.

# *A Torn Love*

She stared long and hard through the stream of tears that fell from her eyes at the lifeless dress that lay on her bed. Her sadness quickly turned to pure hate as she imagined Simone in the dress. She imagined herself pulling and ripping the dress off Simone's body. Shaking her head, she read the handwritten letter again.

"Who in the hell do you think you are?" she asked the lifeless dress, her eyes continuously shifting from the letter to the dress. "You are no one, and I will damn sure prove it to you."

She walked out of the room and carried the letter with her. She needed to do something quickly about the situation. She went to the bar in the den and opened a fresh bottle of dark rum. As she poured her first shot, she read the letter again. The words she read were too passionate and understanding, but she felt no passion and no understanding. She felt nothing but hate.

"Bitch!" she yelled aloud as she tore the letter into pieces. She poured one more shot of the strong, dark substance, swallowed it in one gulp, and went back upstairs to her spacious bathroom. She stared long and hard in the mirror at her worn face. She could not allow the one she truly loved to leave her life so easily. She had to devise a plan. A plan that would bring her the happiness she desired, the happiness she longed for. The happiness she deserved.

As she retuned to her room, thoughts of ripping the dress from Simone danced in her mind again.

"And now the games begin," she whispered softly to herself.

# 13

## *Simone*

The morning after my wonderful evening with Devlin, I sat in my office on cloud nine. My mind was on Devlin Carter from the moment I awoke. I could still smell his cologne, feel his touch on my back, and taste his tongue in my mouth.

After the morning taping, I went back to my office to call Devlin, when Charlene walked in.

"Hey, what's going on with you, Ms. Lady?" she asked as she sashayed into my office carrying a FedEx package in her hand.

"Hey," I said, extra cheery.

She placed the box on my desk.

"Your assistant asked me to give this to you. Is it your dress for Saturday?" she asked.

I read the package and saw Trinity's return address on it.

"I'm not sure. She normally sends packages to my house," I replied nonchalantly, throwing the package on the couch that sat close to my desk.

"I've been following Trinity's work for a while now, and

I love what she does. I think the styles she's done for you are remarkable," Charlene said, taking a seat on the couch next to the package, eyeing it as if she were a kid wishing she could open a gift before Christmas morning.

"Want to do lunch?" she asked.

"Not today. Had a long night. I just want to head home and relax."

After she left my office, I called Devlin and got his voice mail. I left a message, grabbed the package, and headed home.

When I got home, I lay on the blanket that remained on the floor from the previous night. I replayed the entire evening repeatedly until I fell asleep.

When I woke up, I went to my room, grabbed the package off the bed, and decided to open it. It was puzzling that she sent it to the studio instead of my home.

When I opened the package, all of the happiness I had felt in the last eighteen hours disappeared. I grabbed my phone and dialed her number.

"Hellooo," she sang.

"Trinty, what the hell is this?" I yelled.

*Click.*

"No, that bitch didn't!" I shouted, staring at the phone.

I immediately pressed the redial button, and it went directly to her voice mail.

"You need to call me and explain this," I said as calmly as I could.

I went back over to the package and stared at it in disbelief.

"Twenty-five hundred fucking dollars shredded to hell."

I was disgusted and could not believe Trinity had done that. I picked up the shredded dress and dropped the pieces back into the box. Maybe I deserved that from her. I never kept my desire to be with a man a secret, but maybe I was wrong for telling her the way I did. Maybe I was wrong for even involving myself with her in the first place. Maybe I was just selfish and only thought of my own needs and desires.

I looked at the dress one more time and cried myself to sleep.

# 14

## Devlin

*She wanted you. Why didn't you go for it?* I asked myself repeatedly as I drove home.

I could not stop thinking about Simone's body. She showed no shame and exposed her beautiful chocolate breasts when I asked her to remove her camisole. There was a time when I would have jumped on what appeared to be an open invitation, but something told me not to do it. Something deep within made me know that she was something special, and to move slowly.

It was almost three in the morning when I arrived home and I was tired, but I was afraid to go to sleep. Sleep brought dreams, and dreams brought sadness, something that I really did not want at the time.

As I lay in my bed, my manhood reminded me how disappointed he was that I hadn't allowed him pleasurable relief, but my mind agreed that I had made a sound decision.

When I finally woke up, it was twelve in the afternoon. I felt happy, something I had not experienced in a long time. I replayed my evening with Simone in my head. I went into the living room, turned on the TV, grabbed the remote, and hit the forward button until I came to the part of Jacob's DVD that I wanted to hear.

"There is someone out there that's going to be there for you, but there are two people holding you back from receiving her into your life. One of those persons is a pure heifer, no name needed, and you need to dismiss her. The other . . . well, he has to die in order for her to come."

I repeatedly played Jacob's message. I knew the two people he was referring to as having to leave. But was Simone that someone who was going to be there for me?

Thoughts of her enveloped me. I thought about the kiss she and I shared, how I felt connected in ways that I never felt with anyone else.

I drifted off to sleep, fanatisizing about her and the moments we were together, when my phone awakened me. I answered without looking at the ID.

"Hello," I said.

"Hello, Devlin," Leslie answered.

My smile disappeared. "Can you call me later?" I asked.

"I just wanted to know why you didn't have the guts to tell me," she said with attitude. I did not know what she was talking about.

"Tell you what?"

There was a long pause.

"About you and Simone Jackson," she said.

I sat straight up, feeling annoyed.

"Leslie, number one, there is nothing to tell. Number two, even if there was something to tell, you would be the last person who I would tell. What gives you the right to think that I have to report any happenings of my personal life to you?"

She did not respond. We sat in silence.

"Look," I continued. "You have made choices in life that have affected me as well as yourself. I had to learn to deal with it. Now I am suggesting that you learn to deal also." I stood up and walked to the window. Her car was parked behind mine in the driveway.

*She really doesn't give up*, I thought, watching her.

"Devlin, I love you."

I did not respond.

"You know better than me that you could never feel about another woman like you feel about me, just like I could never feel the same love I have for you with any other man."

I had taken all I could. It enraged me that this heifer had the nerve to say that to me.

"Leslie, I chased your ass for over six years. Showed you all the love I knew how to show you, and while you were still seeing me, you accepted a proposal from a man you had just met, then waited over a month to inform me, while we continued to share whatever the hell it was we had. Now you have the audacity to come to me and tell me that you could love no other. You need to go home and sleep in the bed you've made for yourself."

I paused, then walked away from the window and sat back on my couch. "All week long, you've called and come over here unannounced to profess this fucking so-called love, but now the shit is old. I am moving on, and I suggest you do the same."

"Devlin, tell me you don't love me and I will leave you alone," she pleaded.

"Leslie, my love has no bearing on you leaving me alone. For the past several years, you were the only woman I had any kind of emotional or sexual dealings with. I never allowed myself to even think of being with another woman, and now I am realizing more and more each day that my dealings with you have brought me nothing but pain and loss."

"Loss?" she asked. "What kind of loss? To fuck other women?"

She didn't want to understand what I was saying. I had reached my limit with her, and she needed to know there was nothing she could do or say that would allow me to change my mind.

"I lost my dignity dealing with you, and now that I've regained it, I refuse to lose it again. Have a good life." I hung up the phone without saying bye.

I watched her pull slowly out of the driveway. Relief lifted me and I heard Jacob's voice.

*One of those persons is a pure heifer, no name needed, and you need to dismiss her.*

"Brother, she is dismissed," I said aloud as I removed the disc from the DVD player and placed it back in its envelope.

"So what's on your plate for the evening?" Simone asked.

"Well, Stephanie asked me to come over to help plan the services for Jacob's funeral," I said solemnly. It was something that I really did not want to do. "What about you?" I asked.

"I have a speaking engagement tomorrow and Charlene and I are going to look at dresses."

Again, more silence. For the first few days, we had done a lot of talking, but since I left her house the day before, our conversations were awkward.

"Can I ask you a question?" she asked.

"Sure, you can ask me anything."

"Are you attracted to me?" Simone asked softly.

I began to laugh nervously. Of course, I was attracted to her. "Yes, I am very attracted to you. Why do you ask?"

"I was just curious." She paused. "To be honest, Devlin, I am not that experienced with dating."

That did not surprise me at all. I remembered Jacob saying there was something different about her, but he could not pinpoint what it was. After spending time with her myself, I could see how he had come to that conclusion. I could tell something was different about her from most women I had dated, but, just like Jacob, I could not pinpoint what it was.

"Simone, over the past few days, I've come to enjoy our talks and the time we've spent together." I paused and took a sip of water that was sitting on my coffee table in front of me. "I will be honest and say that if this was about six or seven years ago, I would not have left, wishing and wondering what could or would have happened.

"I like you, and I want our relationship to grow and not swell, because when something swells, it's only temporary but when it grows, it's for an eternity."

"I like you too, Devlin," she said, and I could hear a smile in her voice.

Later, I headed to Jacob's house to help Stephanie plan the funeral.

When I walked out of the door, I noticed a burgundy Cadillac Escalade parked in my driveway. As I locked my door, an older man stepped out of the SUV.

"Hello, young man. How are you?" he asked, extending his hand for me to shake.

"I'm wonderful. Thanks for asking," I responded, accepting his hand.

"Is this the Carter residence?"

"Sure is. I'm Devlin Carter," I responded.

He gave me a long, silent stare.

"I—I was an old friend of your grandmother's," he said with a slight smile. "My name is Henry Carlisle."

"It's a pleasure to meet you, Mr. Carlisle. I was about to head out, but if you would like to come in for a few minutes, you are welcome."

He did not respond right away. He continued to give me a strange stare.

"No, son, I won't hold you up. I have been living up in New Jersey for some thirty-odd years now, and recently retired and decided to come home. I was just riding around, getting familiar with the area again, and as I came through here, I thought I would stop by," he said.

I assumed he was coming to see Grammy, so I decided to break the bad news to him.

"Well, I'm not sure if you are aware, but my grandmother died five years ago."

A look of sorrow came over his face.

"No," he whispered. "I wasn't aware. I'm very sorry to hear that."

After a few more moments of his strange staring and odd silence, he climbed back into his truck.

I watched him drive away and wondered who he was. I could not remember Grammy ever mentioning a Henry Carlisle, and he looked too young to be that good a friend of hers.

As I drove to Jacob's house, I had a strange urge to call Simone back, just to say hello. I felt like I was back in seventh grade, when I would call my first girlfriend, Sonya Blake, every minute on the minute. Sometimes I would just call to tell her the time, or to say hello. It was an age of innocence, and the newness of puppy love was better than any one thing the world had to offer. I longed to feel that again. I dreamed of the day that I would feel that again. I had begun to believe I could never open up to a woman again, but along came Simone.

I picked up my phone to call her just as it rang.

*Simone.*

"Hello," I said happily into the phone, realizing that God still remembered me.

# A Thin Line

She walked through the airport wearing dark shades with pure grace. Her black Donna Karan dress, along with the DK shoes, showed those who stared that she was a woman of sheer elegance. Men stared with desire, but they were of no interest to her. They meant nothing.

When she arrived at her designated gate, she took a seat and placed her pocketbook and carry-on on the seat beside her. She removed her shades and placed them inside her pocketbook.

She closed her eyes as she thought about her plans. She still did not have all of the kinks worked out, but she was well prepared to begin.

"Hello, beautiful." A male voice forced her eyes to open to see who was disturbing her thoughts.

"Hello," she responded drily, hoping he would get the hint that she did not want to be bothered.

"Business or pleasure?" he asked, attempting to strike up a conversation.

She stared hard at the tall, dark man. His features were

far from her liking, and she failed to see the need to entertain him.

"Business," she replied as she grabbed her bags and walked away.

She found another available seat far away from the man, but still felt his eyes on her. This was nothing new for her, something that she had become accustomed to dealing with. Some days she would even entertain the men that approached her, but today was not one of those days.

When the ticket agent announced the first-class seating, she went to the gate. Once settled in her window seat, she stared out of it, wondering how successful her plan would be. Would her efforts end in the result she desired?

Her mindset frightened her when she thought about it. Although she felt calm, she knew that somewhere within, she was in a hectic rage. She had just spent over fifteen-hundred dollars on a round-trip ticket across the country, and her flight would be longer than her actual visit. But she had to get the ball rolling quickly if her plan was to work.

The same deep voice interrupted her thoughts again. "Looks like we will be neighbors for the next five hours," the man said as he took the seat beside her.

Her first thought was to find another seat, but that would be impossible.

"Yes, it looks that way," she said drily, hoping that he would notice her tone and would not bother her during their flight.

# 15

# *Simone*

"Praise God and good morning!" My mother had been answering the phone like that since I could remember.

"Good morning, Mother," I said, unsure how she was going to respond to my call.

"Simone Jackson, is that you?"

"Yes, ma'am, it's me." Suddenly, I felt the butterflies in my stomach. I did not know why I had called, but she was heavy on my mind when I woke up.

"Is everything okay? Robert, Simone is on the phone," she yelled to my father.

"Yes, ma'am," I said again, feeling as if I were ten years old. "I . . ." I paused to take a deep breath. "I met someone."

There was a long pause, and then I heard my father pick up the other phone.

"Simone, is that you? For real?" he asked happily.

"Yes, Daddy, it's me for real." It felt good to hear my father's voice.

"Robert, she just said she met someone," my mother began. "Is it a man or a woman?" she asked cautiously.

"It's a man, Mother."

*"Praise God, hallelujah!"* my mother yelled into the phone.

My dad and I remained silent, knowing that once she got into her praise routine, it was going to be a while before anyone else would get a word in.

When she finally came down from her high, I told them both about Devlin. It felt good to talk to my parents, and it felt even better that I was talking about a man to my mother.

"Are you going to church this morning so that you can thank God for delivering you?" my mother could not resist asking before hanging up.

"Yes, Mother, as a matter of fact, Devlin and I are going to church together."

Again, she praised God.

After hanging up with my parents, I looked at the clock. Eight-fifteen AM.

I had just enough time to relax in my tub and reflect on the past six days of my life.

After the taping on the previous Friday morning, I showed Suzette and Charlene what Trinity had done to my dress.

"Bumpkins, if I ever see that Jamaican street hussy again, I will whip that bitch's ass for you," Suzette said with pure and genuine rage.

"So, you are a lesbian?" Charlene asked, confused. She hit her head. "My les detector must be waaaaay off, because I promise you I didn't pick up on that when I met you."

I laughed at the comment.

Over lunch, I told my life story to Charlene. Something

about her made me feel very comfortable. In the matter of a week, I had gained the man of my life and a little sister.

"So," Charlene began, as she took a bite of her spinach salad, "does Devlin know about your recent past?"

My happy mood disappeared.

"No. I don't really know how to tell him," I responded.

Charlene looked at me suspiciously as she chewed her food.

"Simone, I'm the last person to get all up in your business, but you need to tell him. If this crazy-ass bitch would do what she did to your dress, you can best believe she has some other things brewing."

I thought about what she said. Deep down I wanted to believe that the shredded dress was the last I had heard from Ms. Trinity Waters.

After lunch, we spent the afternoon shopping and found a perfect ensemble for my Saturday evening engagement.

I took a quick shower and relaxed on my couch with a bottle of wine, waiting for Devlin's call. Before I knew it, I had dozed off. The next thing I remembered was waking up at four in the morning to the beeping of my cell phone.

*Eight missed calls. Four messages.*

*First message:* "Simone, this is Dev. It is about nine PM and I am leaving Jacob's now. Call me when you get the chance."

*Second message:* "Hey Simone, it's me, Dev, again. It's around eleven. Haven't heard from you and just making sure all is well."

I began to smile from ear to ear.

*Third message:* Click.

*Fourth message:* "You will pay, bitch," the accented woman said.

I deleted the message. I refused to let her bother me. Instead, I touched my lady and thought of Devlin until I fell asleep.

The next morning, I called Devlin to apologize for not getting back to him. He understood and suggested that we meet for breakfast at Shoney's.

"You want to meet at Shoney's?" I asked.

"Best breakfast bar in the world," he responded, laughing before hanging up.

We arrived at Shoney's at the exact same time. He parked his older model Lexus Coupe beside my BMW.

"Nice truck," he said.

"It's a SUV. Ladies don't drive trucks," I said as we embraced one another.

After eating, we remained in our booth for over an hour, chatting and talking about everything. So many times, I wanted to tell him of my past, but I was afraid he would not understand. As we were about to leave, an older man passed our booth.

"Devlin," he said as he reached out his hand.

"Mr. Carlisle. Good to see you again."

Devlin introduced us and as I shook his hand, I noticed that something about this man seemed very familiar to me, but I couldn't place how I knew him. After Mr. Carlisle walked away from us, I noticed Devlin staring at him.

"How do you know him?" I asked.

"Actually, I don't," he said solemnly. "He came by my house the other day looking for my grandmother."

He had told me that his grandmother had died five years ago. I figured having someone come by the house to talk with her after all those years made Devlin curious.

We finally left. Before I got into my car, Devlin grabbed my hand and kissed me in the parking lot of Shoney's. It amazed me that I felt comfortable kissing in public. Not once did I fear people seeing me in a negative light. After our long and passionate kiss, he stared at me with those hypnotizing eyes.

"Do you have any plans for tomorrow?"

"You tell me," I said seductively, hoping he was going to suggest something that I had dreamed about all week: an all-day sexual marathon.

"Would you like to go to church with me in the morning?"

*Awwww*, I thought. But the suggestion still made me as moist as the massage he had given me a couple of days before.

I got out of the tub and prepared myself for my church date with Devlin. My new life was beginning, and I could not think of a better place to begin it than in church with a handsome man.

He arrived promptly at ten-thirty, just as he said he would. Devlin looked as handsome as ever, wearing a very conservative gray suit. His tie was a mixture of several colors with a gray base, but it was his Italian leather shoes that set his ensemble off to a T.

"Hello, pretty lady," he said as he walked in and leaned forward to kiss my cheek. I began to blush.

At church the usher directed us to sit in the front, where I immediately recognized Jacob's entire family. I thought it was very special that they all decided to attend church together the day before his funeral. In addition, a person would never have known that Devlin was not family the way they all interacted with him.

During the service, tears constantly flowed down my face. I felt warmth that I had not felt since college. It was beautiful, and for the first time since I could remember, I felt free.

After church, we went to Jacob's house for dinner. Everyone made me feel as if I belonged.

Devlin never let me out of his sight, and whenever he

was more than a few feet away, I could feel those hazel eyes watching me.

"Simone," Jacob's wife said while tapping me on my shoulder. "Could I speak to you for a moment in private?"

After telling Devlin I would return, Stephanie and I walked upstairs to her bedroom.

"I know you and Dev just met," she began. "But I want you to know that in the past few days, I've never seen him as happy as he is now." She paused, and I saw tears begin to drop from her eyes.

I walked over to hug her, and suddenly I felt as if I wanted to cry also. Once we broke from our embrace, she asked me to have a seat in the sitting area of their bedroom.

"Before Jacob died, he told me not to worry about anything." She paused and tears tumbled from my eyes.

"He made a video for each of us, and believe it or not, he has one for you."

"He has one for me?" I asked, confused. I had only met him once, and that was years ago when I interviewed him.

She gave a slight smile, then handed me the disc.

"If you like, you can watch it here in privacy. I haven't watched it, so whatever it says is something that will remain between you and him." She walked out of the room, leaving me alone to watch the video made specifically for me from her deceased husband.

I placed the disc in the DVD player and sat back in the chair nervously, not having an idea what I was about to witness. Jacob appeared on the screen.

"Hello. My name is Jacob Brown. I know this is strange to you, watching a video of a dead man." He paused and smiled. "But this is something that I felt I had to do. First of all, I want to apologize for us meeting like this, but as I'm sure you may know, our plans in life and God's plan for us are usually not the same." He paused and took a sip of water.

"For over twenty-four years, Dev has been closer to me than my own brother, and I love him more than a brother. He and I have been through some good times, and we have been through our share of bad. Devlin is one of the most outstanding guys I've ever known, and I want nothing but what's best for him." Tears fell from his eyes.

"In the video I made for Devlin, I told him that in my death, someone would come into his life to complete it. I wish I knew for a fact that was true. I told my wife that when and if Devlin brought a woman around, she would know if she was the woman for him." Jacob wiped the tears from his eyes. "I want him to be happy. I want you to be happy with him.

"Since my illness has turned for the worse, Devlin has not come around as often as he used to or as often as I wish he had, but I understand why. He has had to experience a lot of pain and hurt most of his life, and to be around me at this point is too much for him.

"Whomever God has for him, I know she is a true godsend. Be there for him. Be honest with him. Love him, because I will guarantee you that this man will always be there for you. He will always be honest with you, and he will love you more than anyone has and will ever love you."

An uncontrollable stream of tears poured from my eyes like waterfalls. I quickly hit the pause button. I had to regain my composure. I finally understood the full magnitude of Devlin's loss. Jacob was a true friend to him, a true brother.

I wiped my face and hit the play button to listen to his final words.

"Again, I'm sorry for not being able to meet you personally or even to know your name, but as I stated, God has other plans for me now." He paused a final time. "I hope and I pray that you and Devlin will share the love that Stephanie and I were blessed with."

The video ended. I sat there for a few moments and absorbed Jacob's words. It felt like I had held a conversation with him, although I never said a word.

I removed the disc from the DVD player, made a quick stop to the bathroom, and then headed downstairs to find Devlin. He quickly approached me and studied my face. His smile changed to a sheer look of concern.

"You've been crying," he said as he pulled me inside his arms. "Is everything okay? Where were you?"

I looked up at him as more tears fell.

"I was having a talk with Jacob," I said softly.

"You had a talk with Jacob?" he asked, confused.

I showed him the video, his face registered understanding, and we embraced each other again.

# 16

## *Devlin*

"Leslie just left about twenty minutes ago," Stephanie said as I walked in.

"Has Trevor been by yet?" I asked, quickly changing the subject. That was a name that I would not miss hearing.

"I haven't seen Trevor since we left the hospital Wednesday morning. I'm worried about him."

"I am too," I said as she and I walked into the dining room.

I noticed how tired she was as we sat down at the table. I knew the feeling.

"Thanks for everything, Devlin."

"We're family," I said and leaned over to hug her.

Once we were done with the preparations, Stephanie went into the kitchen and brought back two beers.

"So, what's up with you and Simone Jackson?" she asked.

"I think I'm digging her. She has really been a big comfort these past few days," I said with a huge smile on my face.

There was silence. I thought that I had offended

Stephanie with that comment. For years I had secretly envied the relationship that she and Jacob had, and now in his death, someone new had entered my life.

"I miss him, Dev," she said, breaking our silence.

"I know. I miss him too."

I noticed the tears forming in her eyes. I felt them coming in mine as well, but I had to suppress them. I needed to be strong for her.

"I need for you to promise me something," she said as she wiped her tears.

"You name it, you got it."

"I need for you to make sure Li'l J and Cody know their dad. You knew him better than anyone did. Talk to them about what he was like as a boy and tell them what made him into the man that he is." She paused and her voice cracked. "I mean the man that he was."

It was a promise she did not even have to ask me to make. I thought about the day Jacob and Stephanie brought Li'l J home. It was a warm June evening, and Jacob came in the house carrying Li'l J as I held the camcorder, taping every moment.

"Follow me," Jacob commanded. He walked out on the back patio as Stephanie and I followed. He thrust Li'l J to the sky like Kunta Kinte did with his son in the movie *Roots*. I started laughing, and Stephanie yelled at him for raising her newborn child into the sky. He quickly hushed us both up.

"Both of y'all shut the hell up. This is serious business." We both became quiet. "Let us all bow our heads and close our eyes." Again, we both followed his command.

"Dear gracious and kind Father, we come to you now, Father, as humble as we know how, asking you to bestow upon this child your sweet grace and your precious mercy. We pray, oh Heavenly Father, that you will also place prosperity and longevity of life on the parents of this child and on his godfather, to whom you have given your divine authorization to care for this child. We pray, Father, in all these things and more, amen."

When we opened our eyes, I noticed Stephanie had tears in hers. She reached up and kissed Jacob on his cheek.

"Baby, that was so sweet," she said, smiling as she wiped the tears from her face.

"Flesh of my flesh, blood of my blood," he responded.

Two years later when Cody was born, Jacob performed the same ritual. Jacob was truly a man about family.

It was nine PM when I left Stephanie. I called Simone as soon as I got in my car. I got her voice mail.

When I got home, I decided to just relax and think about my week and continue to bask in the vicissitudes of it. I thought about what Stephanie said before I left.

"You of all people deserve happiness," she began as we stood at her doorway. "When Leslie stopped by, I initially thought that she was here out of concern. She really played her game well, until she began asking me questions about you and Simone."

I could tell that she was hurt, and I felt that it was my fault for having had dealings with Leslie.

"Stephanie, I am truly sorry that she came by," I said, trying to ease the pain that Leslie brought.

"Dev, you have nothing to apologize for." A faint smile came across her face. "She told me you kicked her to the curb, and hearing that was like music to my ears. Even before she got married I didn't like that bitch," she said before we hugged and said our good-byes.

Around eleven o'clock, I called Simone again but got her voice mail. I fell asleep.

My ringing phone woke me, but I was happy to see Simone's name on the caller ID. I made plans to meet her for breakfast, hopped in the shower, and dressed.

* * *

While sitting at Shoney's, I still could not believe how good I felt being around her. It had been so long since I had felt complete happiness, and I never knew of a time where I felt this good about a woman so soon.

As we stood outside saying good-bye, a bit of sadness overwhelmed me. I did not want to leave her. A sudden urge to kiss her came over me, and I placed my lips onto hers without caring who saw us.

As we said bye, I asked her to attend church with me the next day, and I was pleased when she accepted.

The next day after church, we all went over to Jacob's house, where there was an abundance of food prepared by members of their church and family.

When Simone and I walked in, folks behaved like I had a major superstar with me. Several people stared at us, and a few of Jacob's old teammates gave me a *How the hell you end up with her?* look. We both mingled with everyone. Stephanie eventually walked over to Simone and after a brief conversation, Simone let me know she was going to have a talk with Stephanie and would be back shortly.

When they walked upstairs, I was tempted to follow, but as soon as they made it up the stairwell, Li'l J came over to me.

"Uncle Dev got him a celebrity girlfriend," he said, smiling as he reached his fist over to me to give him a pound.

"What's going on with you?" I asked.

"I'm doing okay." He paused. "Not used to being around this many people."

I smiled, understanding how he felt. When Grammy died, there were so many people at our small house for days, and half of them I had not seen before her death or again since.

"I watched the video after you left Wednesday. My dad told me if I ever needed anything, you would be there."

"Your dad told you the truth," I said, remembering the promise that I made a long time ago and knowing that I was damn sure going to keep it.

After talking with Li'l J, I walked around and talked with different people. I made a full circle around the crowded house, but was becoming worried because I had not seen Trevor. I was afraid that he was somewhere getting high, hoping that would help him cope with his loss. Trevor was very strong and able to handle things when we were growing up. Somewhere, his strength had decayed and he found it easier to run.

After searching around the house one more time, I noticed Stephanie coming downstairs alone and wondered what had happened to Simone. Every time I tried to make my way to Stephanie to ask her, someone stopped me.

After about thirty minutes, Simone tapped me on my shoulder. When I turned around, I could tell that she had been crying.

"You've been crying," I said with concern. "Is everything okay? Where were you?"

"I was having a talk with Jacob," she said softly.

"You were talking with Jacob?" I asked, confused.

Then she showed me a disc.

"He made you a video too?" I asked, wondering what made him choose her of all people to make a video of himself.

"Yes. He said that it was for the lady that would be there for you."

I stood there in shock. I thought about Jacob's life and how he appeared to have the gift of discernment, and chuckled to myself. Only Jacob.

We went back to Simone's house.

"Would you like to come in for a while?" she asked.

She wanted to play the video for me. I declined at first, but I really wanted to hear what my friend had said to her.

After watching the video, I cried uncontrollably. My tears were not of sadness, but of joy. Joy of knowing that my best friend was still watching over me in his death.

Simone held me until I calmed down. When I quieted, she softly wiped my tears away with her hands. Her touch demonstrated that she possessed a caring spirit.

We sat on her couch for hours with minimal conversation. The TV was on, but we did not really pay any attention to it. We both fell asleep, waking in the wee hours of the morning.

"Let's go lay down," she suggested.

As I followed her to her enormous room, I felt nervous. I was afraid to lie next to her, knowing that my attraction could lead to something that could destroy what we were in the process of developing.

I removed my clothes and climbed into her bed with my T-shirt and boxers on. She walked into the bathroom and returned wearing a long white T-shirt.

My eyes stayed focused on her as she walked to me, and new emotions flooded my mind. When she climbed in beside me, I could smell a hint of perfume.

"Are you comfortable?" she asked.

"Very. Are you comfortable?"

"Very," she replied.

She came closer into me, and I wrapped my arms around her and we both drifted back to sleep.

The next morning, she jumped into the shower. When she reentered the bedroom, she was dressed and ready for the funeral. She decided to follow me to my house.

After leaving her mini-mansion, I wondered what she would think about my modest digs, but once we arrived at my house, that thought quickly left my mind.

"Your house reminds me of my grandmother's house in Alabama," she said as she walked in. "Sometimes I really miss home."

"How often do you visit?" I asked.

"I don't," she whispered sadly. "But I think a visit is soon in the making."

After I finished dressing, we left in her SUV and headed to Jacob's.

Four limousines waited in the front of the house with a convoy of cars behind.

"Simone, you are family now. You will ride with us," Jacob's mother instructed.

The huge church was full with old friends, family, teammates, coaches, and fans. Their attendance, in my opinion, displayed how Jacob had touched many lives in different ways.

I listened to the stories of past coaches and teammates, nervous because I had not prepared a speech of my own. After teaching for many years, I took pride in preparation, but since his death, every attempt to write it ended with me breaking down.

When the pastor called me forward, I nervously walked to the pulpit. The sun crept in through the back windows of the church and I felt a strong peace.

"About twenty-four years ago," I began, "a big kid moved into my neighborhood. Little did we know that a strong bond would form between the two of us.

"Jacob and I experienced a lot of firsts together. We received many whippings together. But Jacob was not just my friend. He was not just my teacher. He was my brother.

"He always possessed the gift to know things, and he didn't mind sharing with you all that he knew." I heard a few people in the congregation agree.

"My grandmother used to always say, 'that boy gots an old soul in him,' and that he did. Today we are not just here to say good-bye; we are not here just to wish him a well journey, but we are here to honor him for his contribution to our lives. I will miss Jacob tremendously, but I know that he is still watching over each and every one of us who crossed his path in some way."

I looked down at him as he lay in state. "I say to you now, my friend, my brother, farewell to you on this earth, until we meet again."

During the procession out of the church, Simone and I walked out hand in hand. When we reached the last pew, I spotted Leslie. Although she was wearing shades, I could feel her eyes piercing me. I ignored her and hoped that was the last time I would ever see her.

We stayed over at Jacob's for a while after the funeral to help Stephanie clean up and manage the crowd. Before leaving, I noticed Simone and Stephanie conversing while sitting on the couch in the family room, and for the first time in the past few days, I actually saw Stephanie smile.

I could not help but think about all the times in the past I had wished that I could bring someone like her around Jacob and Stephanie, and the four of us could all be the best of friends, doing the things that best friends do.

Back at my house, we sat in Simone's SUV, chatting about the events that brought us to where we were. She was the one, the one who Jacob said would be there for me.

"Can you come in for a few?" I asked.

We sat in my living room arm in arm, and, for the first time in years, I felt God's smile shining down on me.

"Am I the lady of your life?" Simone asked, seemingly out of nowhere.

"Simone Jackson, I do believe that you are." Our eyes met, then our lips.

We were all over each other. It felt as if this were my first time ever being with a woman. I traced my tongue around her neck. I carefully tasted each earlobe. I softly caressed her erect nipples and took each one individually into my mouth. She panted hard, yet soft.

"Oh, Devlin," she whispered as she lay on the couch. I eased my tongue to her belly and traced my tongue down her love trail.

*Knock, knock, knock.*

I tried to ignore it. Whoever it was would have to wait.

*Knock, knock, knock.*

Whoever was at the door would not take no for an answer.

I walked over to the door and looked back at Simone to make sure her body was no longer exposed. She gave me a seductive wink.

I looked into the peephole. Mr. Carlisle stood at my door. Because he had known my grandmother, and after seeing him at my house and Shoney's, I felt like I knew him.

I opened the door. He stood there with a nervous smile on his face.

"Mr. Carlisle. How can I help you?" I asked.

I could not help but think of how bad his timing was.

"Sorry to interrupt you, Devlin," he began after noticing Simone. "But I really need to talk to you."

My mind played out two different scenarios. One was to continue what I was doing to the beautiful woman in my life, the other to talk to an old man whom I recently met and had no interest in really knowing.

The choice was easy. I shook my head no, prepared to tell him to come at another time. But he was persistent.

"I won't take up much of your time. I just need a few moments," he insisted.

"Would you like me to leave?" Simone asked.

"No, dear heart," Mr. Carlisle answered. "I will only be a moment."

I invited him in and offered him the seat nearby the door, giving him quick access to exit once he said whatever he felt he needed to say.

He sat in silence and coughed to clear his throat as I rejoined Simone on the couch.

"Can I get you anything to drink?" I offered.

"No, son, I'm fine, thank you." He looked up at me and glanced over at Simone.

"This is not as easy as I thought it would be," he began again as he gave a nervous laugh. "There is no real excuse, Devlin, for me to have waited thirty-two years to do this, but I am your father."

Rage swept through me as I attempted to stand. Simone quickly grabbed my hand when I flopped back down on the couch in shock, staring at Henry Carlisle.

# Part II

## Six Months Later

# 17

# Devlin

"Do you love her?"

"I love her very much," I replied without hesitation.

"Does she love you?"

"She says that she does," I said with a huge smile on my face, thinking about that night three months ago as we lay in bed and she professed her love to me.

"So what's the problem?"

I thought about the question. Why did I feel like there was a problem? Marriage was something that I always wanted, but I had to be sure this was the right thing to do and that we were both ready for the commitment.

"We've only been dating for six months. Don't you think that's too soon?" I asked.

My father's head dropped down and I could see a look of sadness fill his eyes. I understood what that look meant. Over the past few months since I had met him, I had learned Henry Carlisle well. It was signs of the demon that was creeping in from his past.

He took a sip of his beer, and looked up into my eyes.

"Son, love is a funny thing. It doesn't care when it comes." He glanced at his beer. He summoned the server to come over and ordered another round for both of us. He smiled weakly at me, reached into his wallet, and pulled out a picture. He slowly handed it to me.

I stared at the woman in the picture. It was my mother. Grammy had several pictures of her that I had seen over the years, but this one was new to me. I stared at my mother's beauty and sadness threatened to overcome my soul. I wished I had gotten a chance to know her.

"She was only woman I ever loved," he said. "The only woman I ever allowed myself to love."

As we remained in the booth for several moments not saying a word, I thought about the past six months of my life. When Henry told me who he was, my initial thought was to kick his ass, then kick him out. For the life of me, I could not understand how he waited thirty-two years to contact me.

"You want money, don't you?" I asked him, springing from the couch.

"No, son, I don't want your money." He remained seated.

"So, why now?" I asked, standing up again.

"Devlin, calm down," Simone had said as she pulled me back down to the couch for about the fourth time in five minutes. Anger overtook my soul.

"You have been dead to me all my life, and as far as I am concerned, you're still dead," I said.

Henry reached into his jacket, pulled out a stack of envelopes, and placed them on the coffee table. Then he wrote his number on a piece of paper and placed it on top of the letters.

"After reading these, contact me if you feel like you want to talk. That's my number," he said as he walked out the door.

I remained seated beside Simone, staring at the letters. She remained silent. I remained silent.

"This day of all days, he chose this one to fucking tell me this," I whispered, breaking our silence. "He stopped by the house on Friday. Why didn't he tell me then?"

"Maybe the answers are in those letters," she said softly as she rubbed my back, attempting to comfort me.

"He had thirty-two years to write and send me those. There is nothing in those letters that could explain to me why he didn't even bother to mail them," I said.

She reached over, picked up the stack of worn envelopes, and thumbed through them.

"They're all addressed to him," she said softly. "They are from your grandmother."

I looked at each letter. They were all a year apart and all postmarked on the anniversary of my mother's death.

No tears came to my eyes this time. I had cried enough over the past six days to last me a lifetime, and my eyes refused to shed a tear for a man who had been nonexistent in my life.

"Would you like me to stay?" Simone asked as she watched me thumbing through the stack.

I had wanted her to stay, but I also needed some time alone. I needed time to understand why God continued to use my life as an emotional roller coaster.

After Simone finally left, I counted each letter. Twenty-eight, all exactly one year apart, and the last one sent a month before Grammy's death.

*January 15, 1975*
*Dearest Henry,*

*Baby, how you be? I gots the money you sent and started the account for Devlin just like you asked me to do. I knows you doing what you feel is best, but that boy really needs you in his life. Sarah's death was hard on us all. I always tells people that a parent is suppose to die before her child, but we all knows that God has other plans. Ain't that right?*

*I knows that through the years you and I had our differences, but one thing I know for sure is that you loved my Sarah with more love I ever seen a man love a woman. I often think about the day at the hospital when Devlin was born. That look in your eyes told me more than any words can ever say.*

*Well, baby I ain't going to worry your patience any longer. I knows that God will be the strength you need. Just trust in him and be strong. Don't nobody blame you for what happened. God does everything for a reason.*

*Love always,*
*Essie Mae Carter*

I read all twenty-eight letters, and they all pretty much said the same thing. For years, Grammy had told me my mother had died from cancer, but each letter ended with her telling him that he was not to blame. I needed to know more. Why would he feel that he would be the blame for my mother having cancer?

I placed the letters back on the coffee table, then picked up the piece of paper that had his number on it.

"Hello."

"May I speak with Mr. Henry Carlisle, please?" I said with a shaky voice.

"This is," he replied.

"This is Devlin. Devlin Carter. Can we meet tonight?"

After the server brought us another round, my father finally spoke.

"When I see the look in your eyes with Simone, I can see that you have the same feelings for her that I had for your mother." He paused to take a sip of his beer. "When I see the look she gives you, I see the look your mother used to give me. It's real love, son, and don't let time or what you may see as a lack of time, steal that from you."

We sat silently, with the other customers' conversations drifting around us.

"Your mother didn't want to go to the club that night," he began, reminding me of the story that he had told me months earlier. "But I had to insist. Why did I have to insist?" he asked.

"You never told me what happened to the guy that shot her," I said, still wanting to know more than he seemed able to share.

"Son, you don't want to know what happened to him."

After leaving the restaurant with my father, I called Simone.

"Are you on your way over?" she asked.

"And hello to you too," I said, laughing at how eager she still seemed to be with me after these six months.

"Well, are you?" she insisted.

"Yes, baby, I'm on my way."

At her place, I used the key that she had given me a couple of months before. As I walked up the steps, I thought of my father's advice about not letting time steal our love. I walked back to my car and retrieved the package that I had in the glove compartment, placed it in my pocket, and ran back to the house.

All the downstairs lights were off. A glimmer of light from upstairs trickled down the stairwell. I smiled, already feeling the hint of passion roaming though the house as I heard the soft sounds of jazz playing.

As I walked upstairs, I realized that the light and music were coming from her bedroom. When I walked in, she was laying on top of her bed wearing nothing. I quickly removed each item of my clothing, while she stared at me as if she could not wait for me to join her.

I walked naked to the foot of the bed and climbed up. I licked her right foot, beginning at the sole and slowly sucking each toe.

I slowly licked each one of her calves, giving them much-needed attention. Her soft moans told me that she was pleased. I climbed all the way to her, kissing her soft lips and tasting her tongue in my mouth. When I broke away from our kiss, I traced her entire body with my tongue. I softly licked, then sucked, each nipple. My tongue circled her stomach as I made my way to her sweetness. I placed my fingers into her wetness and gently sucked her clit.

"Aaaggh . . . ooohhhh. . . . right there. Yes, yes . . . yes . . . uhhhhh . . . shit . . . damn . . . right there . . . right there . . . right . . . theeere . . . ooohhh . . . I'm cumin' . . . I'm cumin' . . . oooooohhhhhh." Simone twisted and turned as orgasms repeatedly swam across her body. I softly rubbed my hand across her arms and watched her tremble.

After a few moments, she regained composure and jumped on top of me as if she had all the energy in the world. She placed my manhood inside of her sweetness, giving me the feeling of a warm June evening basking in the glory of love. Simone was warm, she was wet, and she was mine.

"I love you, Dev," she said to me, wrapped in my arms, as we both lay there after at least two hours of pleasure.

"I love you too."

"Where do you see us in, say, three years?" she asked.

"Married and with at least one child," I said, half-joking but mostly serious.

"Be for real," she said as she broke away from our embrace and sat up against the headpost of the bed.

"I've never been more real in my life," I answered as I joined her in a sitting position.

She looked directly into my eyes, trying to see if I was telling the truth.

Simone turned on the lamp beside her bed and gave me a gift bag.

"What's this?" I asked.

"Open it."

When I noticed the small box inside the bag, I realized she was about to do the same thing I was going to do. I could not believe it. I smiled uncontrollably. It never ceased to amaze me how she and I seemed to think the same things at the same time. I opened the box and there it was.

"Devlin," Simone began, "will you marry me?"

# 18

## *Simone*

"You're getting married?" my mother asked suspiciously.

"Yes, ma'am."

There was a long pause.

"Simone, you just met that man."

*Damn*, I said to myself. Why had I thought she would find my news as exciting as I did?

"Besides," she began, "we haven't met him yet, and he hasn't properly asked your father for your hand in marriage."

"Mother," I paused, bracing myself to withstand her reaction to the news. "I asked him."

"You did what?" she yelled. "I know I didn't hear what I thought I heard."

I told my mother about the night of both of our proposals. I told her that we were each planning to propose to the other but I beat him to it.

"Simone," she said, "now, you know I am more than thrilled that God has delivered you, and I realize that you lived that sinful lifestyle for all those years, but baby, those funny women have warped your brain silly. Women do not ask men to marry them. The man asks the father first, and then he asks his bride-to-be."

"Mama, I will have to call you back. Suzette just walked in my office," I lied so that I could get off the phone.

Despite my mother, I sat at my desk glowing at the thought of my upcoming nuptials. Charlene poked her head into my office, interrupting my daydreaming.

"Hey, don't forget the interview with *Entertainment Weekly* this afternoon."

"Thanks," I said, and flashed my ring at her. "Since last night I've only had one thing on my mind."

Charlene ran over to my desk and grabbed my hand to get a closer look.

"When did he ask you? Last night? Damn, how many karats is that thing? He went all out on you. This looks like it cost my salary," she rambled in awe.

"Well, actually, I asked him Saturday night," I admitted.

"You asked him?" she said, interrupting. "Well, his ass didn't waste time getting you a ring yesterday, did he?"

"He already had it with him," I said, blushing.

"Get out of here. Well, I am happy for the both of you guys." She paused for a few moments and then a serious look came over her face. "Have you had that talk with him yet?"

"No," I said solemnly, quickly feeling more guilt than I had over the past few months.

"Simone, I know you're getting tired of me saying this, but you really need to tell him. I mean, let's be honest; you have had to change your phone number at least three times a month now." She took a seat on the couch. "You won't be able to use the crazed-fan lie forever, you know? And once I take the news of your engagement to the press and it hits the wire, I promise you some shit will hit the fan."

She was right. I had to tell him. But every time I tried, something always seemed to come up.

"I'm going to tell him very soon. I promise," I said.

Charlene stared at me as if she knew I was lying.

"Um-huh, we shall see," she answered as she walked out of my office.

I thought about the past few months with Devlin. Since the night of Jacob's funeral when his father showed up at the house, our relationship had become closer and closer. I received a crash course of his entire life in the matter of a few short days.

"Simone. Are you home yet?" he had asked as soon as I pulled into my driveway after leaving his house.

"I just pulled in. What's wrong?"

"I just read the letters," he said softly. "I called up Henry and asked to meet with him." He sat quietly for a moment. "Can you go with me?"

I did not hesitate to say yes. I could tell from Devlin's voice how Henry's news had affected him. Thirty minutes later, Devlin had pulled into my driveway to pick me up.

"Are you okay?" I asked.

"I feel like I'm coming into this thing with you with an overload of baggage," he said.

*If anyone has the overload of baggage it's me*, I said to myself.

I didn't respond. There were so many things that I wanted to say, but there were so many things going on with him that I felt that my past situations could wait.

"Where are we meeting him?" I asked.

"He gave me the directions to his house," he said, chuckling. "He actually lives about four blocks from here."

My subdivision had the lowest-priced homes in the area, so I knew that four blocks away were the million-dollar homes. His father lived in the gated section of my community.

Once we arrived at the gate, the security officer called to make sure that we had clearance to come through.

"Damn," Devlin whispered. "He seems to have done good for himself."

I did not say a word. I thought about Devlin's earlier anger when he had thought his father wanted money. I was curious as to what were in those letters that had given him a sudden change of heart.

We found the house and pulled into the driveway as motion-sensor lights illuminated the place. Devlin parked the car but remained seated as if he had changed his mind. I grabbed his hand.

"You know, it's something about that," he said as he lifted our hands in the air. "It's comforting for me."

I smiled and pecked him softly on his cheek.

"Come in, come in," Henry instructed as he opened the door. I was amazed at the decor.

"Mr. Carlisle, who decorated your home?" I asked.

I knew under the circumstances that my question was inappropriate, but I could not help myself. His home was beautiful.

"I had a young lady from New Jersey come down," he answered as we sat in his living room.

"It looks as if life has treated you fairly well," Devlin stated, breaking the long silence.

Mr. Carlisle gave an uneasy smile and leaned forward in his chair.

"Depends on what you consider to be fairly well," he replied.

More silence. Both of them stared at each other, waiting to see who would speak first. I wanted to say something to help start the conversation, but my role was just to comfort Devlin, so I remained silent.

"I read the letters that Grammy sent to you," Devlin said.

"We both wanted the best for you, Devlin."

"For years Grammy told me that my mother died from cancer," Devlin's said, his voice cracking.

"For years before your mother died, your grammy viewed me as a cancer."

"You killed my mother?" Devlin asked as he stood up from the chair in sudden rage.

Mr. Carlisle never blinked an eye. He remained calm and sat back in his chair.

"For years, I thought I did," he began. "For years, I blamed myself for that night. For years, I never thought that I would be able to face you like a man."

Devlin sat back down.

"What night?" he asked.

"The night I proposed to your mother," he said softly with sadness in his eyes.

I thought about the first day that I had met him, when Devlin and I were eating breakfast, and how familiar he looked.

He was a very distinguished and attractive older man. His salt-and-pepper hair was cut low and his mustache was neatly trimmed. Moreover, he had hazel eyes, just like Devlin.

"Please excuse my manners," Mr. Carlisle said, standing. "Can I offer you anything to drink?"

He returned with a beer for himself and Devlin, and a glass of wine for me.

"What happened that night?" Devlin asked.

Mr. Carlisle stared in Devlin's eyes, then turned to me. I believed that he could not face Devlin.

"Two months after you were born, my uncle asked me to come up to New Jersey and work in his dry cleaning store. I wanted to take you and your mom with me, but your grammy wouldn't allow it. So I went alone, vowing to come back to get you both when I got myself situated." He paused and sipped his beer.

"By the time you had turned two, my uncle opened his second store that I was going to run," he said, closing his eyes. "I always wanted to be a businessman and your mom wanted to go to school and become a teacher. I was making both of our dreams happen." He opened his eyes and looked at Devlin.

"By that time, I had finally convinced your grammy that I could provide for my family, and I came back to get you. After your mother accepted my proposal that evening, she wanted to stay home, but I insisted that we go out to celebrate." He closed his eyes again and his face showed his pain.

"Clarence Robinson, we called him Spanky. He had a thing for your mother. While I was in New Jersey, he tried on a number of occasions to gain her attention, but to no avail. He came into the club and started a fight with me. When he grabbed for your mother, I knocked the shit out of him, embarrassing him in front of everyone. He left after that.

"On our way to my car, I heard a loud noise and saw a sudden flash of light coming from in front of us. Cross-eyed son of a bitch was aiming at me, but when he realized he missed, he ran away and I chased after him but didn't catch up to him.

"When I walked back over to your mother, I saw her lying on the ground, then I saw the blood. By the time we got your mother to the hospital, she was gone. Two hours later, I headed back to New Jersey, where I remained until a month ago."

*Knock, knock, knock.*

The knock on my office door tore me from my memory.

It was Charlene and the interviewer from *Entertainment Weekly.*

After the interviewer left, Charlene told me that she wanted to get started on the press release for Devlin and me. Before she walked out the door, she turned around and looked at me.

"I know you don't want to hear this, but the longer you wait on telling him, the worse the situation could get," she said and then walked away.

She was right. I knew Devlin would understand, but I just wanted to believe that my past had no bearing on my future.

# 19

## *Devlin*

"Uncle Dev, you're rich, right?" Cody asked me.

Since Jacob's death, I had picked him and Li'l J up every Wednesday and I spent a few hours with them. Now that it was summer, I tried to have them all day.

"That's what they tell me. Why?"

"You don't act rich," he responded with the innocence of a child.

"Okay, so tell me, how is rich supposed to act?"

"Well," he started, looking up in the air as if he were thinking hard. "For one, your house doesn't look rich. It's tiny. My room is bigger than this. And your car, it's kind of old. You don't even have any fly rims on it."

I laughed. "Well, yes, my house is small, and my car is old, but can you tell me, what does that have to do with being rich?" I quizzed.

"I mean, I always thought people with money had big things and always drove new cars."

"Dummy, that ain't got anything to do with being rich," Li'l J butted in as he walked back into the living room carrying pizza for him and his brother.

"Li'l J, how many times do I have to tell you to stop calling your brother a dummy?" I asked authoritatively.

"I'm just saying, Uncle Dev, everybody knows that you don't have to have a lot of stuff just because you have money," Li'l J said before he stuffed his face with pizza.

"No, Li'l J, everyone doesn't know that. We live in a society that's full of illusions," I said.

"What's an illusion?" Cody asked.

"Du—" Li'l J began and then smiled at me. "Dearest little brother, an illusion is the state or fact of being intellectually deceived or misled."

Cody still looked confused, but I was very impressed with Li'l J's definition.

"It sounds as if someone has been studying. Your mom tells me that your grades have picked up big-time over the past couple of years."

"Yes, sir, they have. She said you used me as your guinea pig," he said, sticking his chest out, showing that he was proud of himself.

Li'l J, along with my students, were my guinea pigs. I tried out the methods and material that I developed on them and made sure that it not only helped students learn, but they also retained the information and enjoyed learning at the same time. "I got all A's in everything except science," he boasted.

After eating pizza, we drove over to my father's house. He was always glad to have the boys over and, although they had a pool at their house, they loved his pool the most. It looked more like a lagoon than a regular pool, with large rocks and a waterfall. I had to admit that my father's house was one made from dreams. It reminded me of the house I wanted to give Grammy.

As we walked up the walkway, I thought of all the years I had spent with Grammy. I had never known her to work, but we always had everything we needed. When she died, a lawyer came by the house to discuss her estate.

"She left me what?" I asked, not believing what I was seeing or reading.

"Mr. Carter, it was exactly four hundred and fifty-two thousand dollars and thirty-three cents," the young black attorney said as he read off the amount.

"Where did she get that kind of money? Are you sure you are talking about my Essie Mae Carter?"

"Yes, I am very sure," he said with a smile, then handed me a check, shook my hand, and left.

Six months ago, when I first met my father, all those years of wondering where the money came from ended.

"Where's baby girl at?" my father asked as we walked in, referring to Simone.

"She's on her way over. She just called before we got out of the car."

Li'l J and Cody quickly gave my father a pound, changed into their trunks, and jumped in the pool.

I took a seat under the shaded patio as my father went into the kitchen to retrieve drinks. Once he returned, he took a seat next to me and we watched Li'l J and Cody play in the pool.

"Big Unc Henry?" Li'l J yelled as he was about to jump off one of the rocks that lined the pool. "Can I bring my girlfriend over here next time to go swimming?"

My father and I both laughed.

"Li'l J, you and any of your friends are welcomed here anytime," my father said. But his smile quickly faded and that look of sadness returned.

"What's wrong?" I asked.

"All is well, son," he said as he took a sip of his drink. "All is well."

I had learned over the months since we met that he

often had those moments of sadness. It usually came when I brought the boys over, or if he, Simone, and I were together.

"Can I ask you a question?" I asked.

"Devlin, you know you can ask me anything."

I paused for a moment, unsure of how he would react. But the question burned inside my mind since our first real conversation.

"Why did you never marry anyone else?"

He sat in silence for several moments. I thought that he was not going to answer, and I didn't want to pry.

"How long did you say you've known Simone?" he asked.

"About six months, going on seven," I replied.

"And you love her, right?"

"Very much," I said.

"Well, son,"—he paused to take a sip of his drink—"multiply the time and love you have for her by thirty-six years."

I understood. He was sixteen when he met my mother, and he was twenty-two when she died, and he had been in love with her the entire time. No one else could fill that void.

"So, Dad, are you telling me that you haven't had sex in over thirty years?" I asked, trying to create some humor.

"We were talking about love, son, not sex." We both laughed.

I watched the boys play and thought about how hard things had to be for my father during all those years. He had become a very successful businessman, and had all the money that one man could hope for, but he had lost what he loved the most.

I thought about the similarities in our lives. I had gained riches and still was not happy.

"You don't know how often I replay that night in my head," he said. "I wish I could go back in time, just twenty-five seconds before it all happened, and allowed myself to jump in front of your mother and take the bullet that was meant for me."

We were preparing to leave my father's house, but Simone had not yet arrived. As soon as I grabbed my phone to call her, music blasted throughout the house. It was Al Green's "Love and Happiness."

"Where the hell did that come from?" I asked my dad as I searched the house to see who had turned on the stereo.

"Hey, if they can do the ring tones for a phone, why not do one for my doorbell?"

I shook my head and laughed.

"Sorry I'm late. Something came up at the studio," she started. "I know I should have called and I apologize," she continued as she kissed me.

"It's cool. Just about to take the boys home. Want to ride?"

We dropped her SUV off at her house and took the boys home. On our way back, she was more quiet than usual. Over the past few weeks, I had noticed that every so often she seemed to drift off into her own little world.

"Is everything okay?" I asked.

"Yes."

"Are you sure?" Her short answers concerned me. She usually talked my ears off.

"Yeah, I'm sorry. Had a long day, that's all."

I did not pry, but I could not help but think of how on top of the world she appeared when we talked earlier, and now she seemed like someone or something had brought her down from her high.

"Do you have any plans for the weekend?" she asked suddenly.

"No different than usual. Why?"

"Would you like to go to Alabama to meet my parents?"

"Of course I would. You know I still need to ask your father for your hand in marriage," I said jokingly.

When we arrived back at her place, she still seemed somber.

"Let's take a shower," she suggested.

Our showers and baths together had become one of my favorite pastimes. They were not always sexual, but they were very sensual. As she lathered my body, I closed my eyes, and the thought of my mother and father coming out of a club flashed through my mind.

I thought about my father's comment about going back seconds earlier and jumping in front of the bullet that killed my mother. I understood how he felt. In less than a year, I knew that there was nothing Simone could do that would lessen my desire to be with her for a lifetime. My love for Simone could last as long, if not longer, than the love my father still held for my mother.

In bed I could still sense something was bothering her. I wrapped my arms around her and kissed her softly on her neck.

"Devlin," she whispered. "Do you really love me?"

"Baby, of course I do," I said, becoming more concerned. "Why would you think I don't?" I kissed her again on her neck.

"All my life I dreamed and prayed for a man like you and now that you are here, I'm afraid I would do something to make you leave me," she said softly.

I thought about what Jacob told me a week before he and Stephanie got married. He said she questioned him the entire week about his love for her. He told me that

Stephanie was having wedding-bell jitters, second-guessing his love.

I held her tightly to assure her that I was never letting her out of my life.

"There is nothing you can do to make me want to leave you, and I will do everything in my power to make sure you never leave me," I said. I gently sucked her neck and her entire body until I reached her sweetness, which I loved to taste.

# *A Love TKO*

She climbed out of the bed, walked over to the patio doors of the spacious bedroom, and looked out over the beautiful California beaches.

"Lovely, isn't it?" the voice said seductively as the soft kisses landed on the nape of her neck, slightly startling her.

"Yes, but I've seen better," she responded solemnly as she turned to her lover and returned the kisses.

"We must take a trip very soon," her lover said as she removed herself from the loving embrace and was led back to the bed.

"That sounds like a great plan. I really could use a real vacation," she answered.

"I tell you what. Once I complete this current project, we will fly anywhere you desire," her lover said with pure excitement in her voice.

It was late in the afternoon when her lover left the condominium, and she knew that she would be alone for the next several hours. She walked over to the bar and pulled out the bottle of dark Jamaican rum, then got a glass, and brought the entire bottle to the couch, where she had decided to perch and watch TV for the remainder of the afternoon.

"Hmm," she said to herself as she thumbed through the DVD collection to find something to occupy her mind.

Later that evening, she heard her lover return.

"I received a call from my manager and I need to fly to the East Coast immediately," she said as her lover walked through the door. "How about you join me there next weekend?"

"I think that would be a wonderful thing," her lover said with a huge smile on her face.

"I think so too. I think so too."

She arrived in Charlotte. She had revised her plan twenty times or more and knew exactly how she was going to gain her love back. It was only a matter of time now, and she was ready to begin the execution of her plan.

# 20

## *Simone*

"Devlin, are you asleep?" I asked, but received no answer.

As I lay in his arms, tears that I held all day were finally stealing their way out of my eyes.

"Devlin," I tried calling again. He still did not respond.

I continued to lie in silence, wishing I had not waited so long, wishing I had revealed to him more about my past months ago.

"Why didn't I tell him?" I whispered.

My day had started out wonderfully. Charlene and I met in my office after the morning taping, something that had become part of our weekly agenda.

"The way you have this written out, you would think I was royalty or something," I said, smiling from ear to ear as I read the press release concerning our engagement.

"You don't know?" she laughed. "Girl, around here, you are royalty. In less than three months, you've taken a popular local talk show and made it a number-one national show in its time slot."

"Well, don't count yourself out, Charlene. Your hard work had a lot to do with it as well."

She smiled at my compliment. But her work went beyond the compliment I had given her.

Charlene was a true workhorse. She made sure that I received any exposure she could muster up. Not only was she good at her job, but she had also become a great friend.

After going over the press release, we had our lunch delivered to the studio.

"Simone, I've got to tell you. I am seriously jealous of you," she said with a slight smile.

"Why?" I asked as I studied her face.

She stared at me long and hard before she answered.

"Well, I guess *jealous* is really not the right word." She paused. "I mean, I am jealous, but not to the degree of silliness." She paused again. "Did that make sense?"

"Not really," I said, smiling, trying to understand where she was coming from.

She looked up into the sky as if she were hoping that the words she wanted to say would fall down from the ceiling.

"Little girls grow up having lavish dreams. Dreams of great careers, beauty, and most importantly, love," she explained.

"You have a great career and you are gorgeous," I said, interrupting her thoughts.

"But I don't have love," she said.

There was a knock on my door and she fell silent as our lunch was delivered. I recalled the past few months of our relationship. Our conversations consisted of my life. I never took the time to get to know what was going on in hers.

"I meet men," she continued when the room was once again empty. "But ninety-five percent of the ones I meet ain't hitting on jack shit."

We both laughed. "That man loves you, Simone, and you love him. It didn't take either one of you long to figure that out early. That's what I mean by being jealous. I guess that is why I give you such a hard time about not telling him about your past. I know it wouldn't matter to him." She grabbed what remained of her lunch and walked toward the door.

"I know you haven't actually heard from Trinity over the past few months with the exceptions of the hang-ups, but something about her makes me nervous for you, makes me nervous for Devlin. Just be careful."

I thought about everything Charlene had said. She was right; my past wouldn't matter to Devlin, but he would feel as if I betrayed him because I waited so long to tell him after he was so up-front with me.

My assistant buzzed me.

"Simone, you have a call from a Carmen Rinehart-Mitchell. Would you like for me to take a message?" she asked.

"No, please send it through," I said, excited to speak with my old college roommate.

It had been about eight years since Carmen and I had last spoken at a convention in San Francisco. She had moved there immediately after graduation to be, as she stated, near more people like her.

"What's up, Carmen?" I said excitedly.

"It's all about you, from what I've been hearing and seeing. How have you been?" she asked.

"I've been wonderful. So tell me, what's the deal with the two last names?"

"Simone, believe it or not, I'm married now," she said gleefully.

*Is it a man or woman?* I thought, clearly hearing my mother's voice in my head.

I heard her giggle.

"And before you ask, yes, it's to a man."

"Congratulations, Carmen. I am so happy for you. When did all this happen? Why didn't you invite me to the wedding?"

There was a long silence.

"Simone . . . I . . . I basically called you today to apologize."

"Apologize for what?" I asked. I could not think of anything she had ever done to me that would cause her to have to apologize.

"When we were in college, I was confused," she said, then cleared her throat. "I introduced you to a confusing lifestyle and for the past few years, that has haunted me."

I really did not know what to say. I never blamed her or anyone for the choices I made in my life. After telling me all about her husband, Mark, and their one-year-old son, Mark Jr., I felt tension ease from my mind. I figured that if Carmen and Mark could find happiness, Devlin and I could too.

"Does he know about your past?" I asked.

"Since the first day we met. When I met him, I knew he was someone special. I couldn't see not being honest with him about anything."

Suddenly, the tension quickly returned and invaded my mind. I fell silent.

"Simone, are you there?" she asked.

"Yes," I said softly. "I'm still here."

Then I heard a baby's cry.

"Simone, can you hear my son? That's my cue to go be a mommy. Can you believe it?"

I smiled.

"Honestly, Carmen, yes I can."

"Look, Simone, again I want to apologize. There was no

excuse for me coming on to you the way I did. I knew that your curiosity was simply that, curiosity. Please stay in touch, okay?"

I hung up, knowing I had to do what I should have done months ago.

"What's up, baby?" Devlin said as he answered the phone.

"It's all about you, my love. What are you up to?"

"Li'l J, Cody, and me just pulled into Pop's driveway. Are you coming over?"

"I will be there within an hour," I said.

I hung up the phone and prayed to God, hoping that He would give me strength to come clean about my past to the man I was building a future with.

As I was about to walk out of my office, my assistant brought a package. There was no return address, and I initially assumed it was something from Devlin. He often sent me gifts to my office or at home.

I smiled from ear to ear, wondering what it was. When I finally opened the box and removed all of its wrappings, I screamed so loud that everyone outside my office ran in to see what was wrong.

"Simone," Charlene said, grimacing as she looked inside the package. "We need to do something about this bitch and soon."

Suzette agreed.

All night I tried to tell him about everything. All night I wanted to tell him everything, but his last words before making love to me for some reason scared me as well.

"There is nothing you can do to make me want to leave you, and I will do everything in my power to make sure you never leave me."

Those words continued to play in my head, but I could

not help but wonder if he would really mean that once I told him.

I thought about our upcoming weekend trip to my parents' home. I had to tell him before he met my mother. She had a bad habit of saying the wrong things at the wrong times, and the last thing I needed was for her to be the one to mention my past to him.

"Why, Simone? Why didn't you tell him earlier?" I whispered softly as he held me close to him.

Would he forgive me for not being open with him?

Carmen had been honest from the very beginning with her husband. Why hadn't I done the same thing?

My mind was so full of thoughts that I could not sleep. It was 4:02 AM.

I tried to fall asleep, but every time I closed my eyes, all I could see was the content of the package Trinity sent to my office. A dead black rat with a note attached: *Dead rats die unnoticed!*

# 21

## *Devlin*

I woke up alone in Simone's bed around eleven-thirty the next morning. She had left hours earlier. I thought about her mood the day before. What was going on with her? Yesterday's mood was the first time I had seen her like that since we had known each other.

Her phone rang. I looked at the caller ID.

*Unavailable.*

It was probably Simone calling me from her office. I immediately answered.

"Hello, Jackson residence."

*Click.*

The hang-ups were beginning to get on my nerves. They started at her house and cell phone about four months earlier and at my house about three weeks ago.

"Overzealous fans," she said, easily dismissing it.

In my life experiences, hang-ups were someone trying to get your attention. It had been months since I had heard from Leslie, so I assumed it was her.

On my drive home, my cell phone sang. Simone was calling me.

"Hey," I said, happy to hear from her.

"I love you," she said happily.

Her mood appeared to have improved.

"I love you too."

"Devlin, I was sitting here doing some thinking about this weekend," she started. "Let's ask your dad to drive down with us."

"We're going to drive?" I asked.

"I thought a drive would be a good thing for the three of us. It's only about a six-hour drive."

It had been years since I had been on a road trip. When we were kids, Jacob's parents always invited me on summer trips to Florida to visit their family.

I used to look forward to the trips because Mr. and Mrs. Brown always treated me like one of their own.

They would also invite Grammy, but she always declined, saying that long trips gave her the boonts.

"What are the boonts?" I finally asked her.

"Baby, the boonts is when you gots to go sit on the stool."

"Simone, a road trip sounds like a great plan to me," I said as I pulled into my driveway. "I will give Dad a call in a few and see if he would like to go."

I noticed the door to Grammy's room was open when I entered the house. The lamp that sat beside her bed was on. I knew I hadn't gone into her room the day before. I checked the entire house for signs of a break-in, but found nothing.

I returned to her room to turn the light off and noticed her Bible on the nightstand next to her bed.

It had been sitting in that same spot since the day she died; it seemed to have drawn me to it.

I picked up the Bible and a white envelope fell out. My father's name was on it.

I stared at it, wanting to read it but not daring to open it. Whatever the letter contained, it was between him and her.

"Hey, son, what's going on?" my dad asked as he walked in the door.

"I'm going down to Alabama with Simone this weekend to meet her parents." I paused. "Would you like to ride with us?"

A huge smile came over his face.

"You don't think she would mind?" he asked.

"She's the one that suggested that you go."

He grinned like he was holding a lottery ticket.

We were eating lunch together at Backyard Grillin', and I handed him the letter.

"Your grandmother was a wise woman," he said as he sadly stared at the letter. "She had so much insight."

"Yes, she did," I whispered.

A look of worry came over his face

"You want me to read this now, don't you?"

"No, sir, you should read it when you feel the time is right for you," I said.

He stared at the letter for a few minutes, folded it, and placed it inside his shirt pocket.

I headed back home after dinner. On my way back, I still wondered why Grammy's light was on in her room.

"You are referring to this coming Tuesday?" I asked Simone, knowing she had to be joking with me.

"You still owe me an appearance on my show, so why not Tuesday?" she asked with a huge grin.

"Do I have a choice?"

"Nope," she said, then kissed my lips.

Simone had come straight to my house to tell me about her and Charlene's big plan.

"And what am I supposed to do? Just sit on your stage and smile?"

"Do you need the writers to script something for you?" We both laughed.

"Okay, I will be on your show," I said, already feeling nervous.

We had never rescheduled my original appearance. I had spent the last few months getting to know my father, instead. Now when they finally decide to do it, it was to announce to the world that we were getting married.

"So what did Henry say about the trip this weekend?" she asked.

"He suggested that we drive his Escalade."

"Well, I made hotel arrangements in Montgomery. I reserved one for him as well," she said with a huge smile on her face.

"We're not staying at your parents?" I asked.

She gave me a look that said I must have been out of my mind for even thinking that.

"Sweetie, I'm doing good to even go back home," she said with a hint of sadness.

"So how are things with you and her these days?"

She got up from the couch and walked into the kitchen to get a bottle of water out of the refrigerator. I followed.

"Okay, I guess," she answered, but she sounded unsure. "We are getting there."

"Well, that's good," I said.

Months ago Simone told me about her estranged relationship with her mother. She really did not tell me much of what caused their strain, but I still did not agree with her for not speaking with her mother for years.

"You know what, Devlin?" she said when I gave her my feelings on the matter. "My mom has always wanted me to be what she wanted me to be. She tried to hold me down all my life. When I was finally able to break free, I did."

"Her ways may be wrong for you, but she's still your mother. I just believe that regardless of what has happened, family should stand by family," I said sternly.

"You know what? I really do not want to talk about this anymore. You just wouldn't understand."

That statement hurt like hell. I knew she meant no harm, but insensitivity had shown its ugly head. I put on my shoes, and I grabbed my keys and headed toward the door.

"You're right, Simone. I would not understand. I never had the chance to know my mother."

I was about to head out the door when I noticed her eyes had begun to fill with tears. I had not intended to make her sad. She had something that many people didn't, and I wanted her to see that family was still family.

"You two may not get along, but at least you have each other," I said as I walked back toward her and wrapped my arms around her.

"You're right, Devlin," she whispered.

*Ring. Ring.*

We both had dozed off on the couch when the phone woke us up.

"Hello," I answered without looking at the ID.

"Devlin, this is Stephanie."

I looked over at the clock.

One-fifteen AM.

I jumped up. Something must have been wrong.

"What's wrong, Stephanie?"

I could hear trouble in her voice and loud banging in the background.

"It's Trevor. He just showed up knocking on the door, yelling for Jacob to answer."

"I'm on my way," I said.

I told Simone it would be best if she stayed at home. I

knew Trevor as well as I knew Jacob. What renal failure had reduced Jacob to, drugs had reduced Trevor to.

The police were already there when I arrived. Trevor sat on the steps with his hands handcuffed behind his back, crying.

"I just want to see my brother," he cried when he saw me. "I just want to see him one more time."

The officers told me that Stephanie did not want to press charges, but if he did not calm down, they would have to take him in for disturbing the peace.

I sat down beside him and we sat in silence for a few moments. After he appeared to be relaxed, the officers released the handcuffs.

I looked long and hard into his face and realized that he wasn't high at all. "What's going on, Trevor?" I asked.

No one had seen him since the night Jacob died. He did not even show up for the funeral. We were all worried about him.

He continued to sit in silence for a few more moments before answering my question.

"I had to go away for a while," he started. "The night Jacob died, I knew for him, for them boys, I had to go away and get myself together."

"You were in rehab?" I asked, surprised.

He shook his head yes.

"I admitted myself that morning. I thought they were going to let me go to the funeral. If I had known those sons of bitches were going to make me miss my baby brother's funeral, I wouldn't have gone," he said through his tears. "I just want to see him one more time, Dev. Just one more time, that's all."

After the police realized that he was calm, they left. Stephanie sat on the other side of Trevor.

"Trevor, where are you staying?" Stephanie asked, wiping away her own tears.

"Nowhere, really. All the places I can go I know won't be safe for me."

"You stay here as long as you need," she told him.

"I can't do that."

"Yes, you can," she said, refusing to take no for an answer. "You're family."

We went into the house and Stephanie instructed him that he could sleep in Jacob's hideaway room. I walked up with him.

When I entered the room, I suddenly remembered Jacob's request and the package that was in the safe for Trevor. Without a doubt, this was the time for Trevor to have it.

I retrieved the key from my wallet and walked over to the safe. Inside was an envelope and a small metal box safe.

Jacob left him a video as well. Trevor stared at the disc and the metal safe. We both knew what was in the safe.

"I'm going to leave you alone with your brother," I said, walking toward the door.

"Dev," he called.

"What's up?"

"You remember what's in this little safe, don't you?"

"Yeah, and you do too," I replied with a smile.

"I thought he would have given all of his championship rings to you," he said.

"Why? He always said that you were the reason he got them."

Then I left, allowing him to have his last conversation with his brother.

# 22

## *Simone*

"And that's a wrap," Steven, my director, yelled as I rushed offstage trying to get to my office.

I had less than two hours to get home and meet Devlin and Henry so that we could get on the road. I usually stuck around the set for a few moments to sign autographs and answer questions, but there was no time for that today.

A couple of audience members made their way to the stage just as I was about to walk away.

"Simone," a little old white woman who appeared to be in her sixties said, "I love your show so much."

"Thank you so much. I appreciate that."

"And your hair is always so beautiful," she said, smiling.

I returned the smile as I signed a piece of paper for her.

"Is Trinity Waters still your stylist?" a black woman who appeared to be in her late thirties asked me. Just hearing Trinity's name made me feel nervous.

"No, she's not," I responded drily, handed her an autograph, and then instructed one of the production assistants to get me to my office.

As I sat at my desk, I wondered about my mother's promise to me. When I called her earlier in the week to inform her that my future husband and father-in-law would be accompanying me home, I had my father make her promise to be on her best behavior.

"I'm always on my best behavior," she said to my father while I was on the other end.

"Estelle . . ." My dad usually called my mother Stelle, but he would say her whole name when he was serious.

"I believe in telling people what God says is right," she responded.

"Estelle," my dad said again louder.

"I just don't understand why I—"

"Baby, your mother will be just fine," my dad assured me as he cut off whatever it was she was about to say.

"When will you be back? Sunday?" Charlene asked as she walked with me to my SUV.

"Yeah, we'll be back sometime in the evening."

"Okay, cool. See if you can talk Devlin into coming by on Monday morning so that we can get some shots of you guys together."

The trip home was actually refreshing. I enjoyed driving places instead of flying. Driving allowed me an opportunity to see the sights and relax my mind.

"I hate driving through Atlanta," Devlin said as we sat waiting on traffic to move. "Makes no difference what time you come through here, it's always backed to hell."

Henry slept in the backseat. The resemblance of Henry and Devlin was remarkable. As I looked back at him, I envisioned how Devlin would look in his golden years.

I noticed my father's Cadillac parked in the hotel parking lot.

"My parents are here," I whispered softly.

I had told them I would call once we arrived. I knew my mother probably insisted on them being here. I scanned the lobby but didn't see them anywhere.

"Mr. and Mrs. Carter, your room number is four-twenty-two. Mr. Carlisle, you are in four-twenty-four," the overly enthusiastic clerk said.

It made me smile to hear *Mr. and Mrs. Carter*. I reserved our rooms under that name to hide my identity while at home. With everything that had been going on over the past few months with Trinity, I did not want to take any chances on her ruining a weekend with my family.

As we were about to head to our rooms, the clerk stopped us.

"Ma'am, has anyone ever told you that you favor Simone Jackson?"

"No, never," I said as I attempted to walk away.

"Well, you really look just like her. I hear she's from this area," she said, attempting to have a conversation.

"She's very attractive. Thanks for the compliment," I said.

"It's kind of funny. An older couple checked in earlier, instructing me to give Ms. Jackson their room number when she arrived. I naturally assumed it was you coming in under an alias. We get a lot of that here."

I stopped in my tracks. They were not supposed to stay in the hotel. I told my mom that once we settled we would drive down to Union Springs. I walked back to the counter.

"What's the room number?" I asked.

"So you are Ms. Jackson?"

"Yes, I am. Now, can you please tell me the number to their room?" I asked, becoming agitated.

"They're in room four-thirty."

"Shit," I whispered to myself. Leave it to my mother to request a room nearby.

When we reached the floor, I noticed my mother pacing the hallway. When she spotted me, she ran and hugged me as if something was wrong.

"Are you all okay?" she asked with tears streaming down her face.

"Mother, we're fine. What's wrong?"

She seemed relieved. My father emerged from the room.

"Stelle, I told you that it was probably just a crank call," he said. My curiosity was seriously piqued.

"What crank call?" I asked.

My mother looked at me, then at Devlin and Henry.

"Pardon our manners," my father began as he extended his hand to Henry, then Devlin. "I'm Robert Jackson and this is my wife, Estelle."

"It's a pleasure to meet you," Devlin said. "If you don't mind me asking, what type of call did you receive?"

I realized that my mother's comment had piqued his curiosity as well. My mother was always one to overexaggerate, so I knew the call was not as crucial or alarming as she made it out to be.

"Mom, we're going to go to our rooms and put our things up. I will knock on your door when we're done, and we all can go get something to eat," I said as I pushed her toward her room.

"Wonder what type of call they received?" Devlin asked me.

"I told you how my mother could be. Did I not?" I said, more concerned about the call than I wanted him to know.

"Yes, you did. But still, something about that just doesn't seem right."

He was right. When my mother first mentioned it, the first person that came to mind was Trinity.

"Baby," I started, not really knowing what to say. "My . . . my mother can honestly be overdramatic at times. I'm sure the call wasn't anything."

I did my best to hide my own fears from him, but after the dead rat incident and all of the hang-ups, I really did not know what to think anymore.

After we freshened up, we met my parents and Henry in the lobby to go to dinner.

As we walked to Henry's SUV, my mother realized that she had left her purse in the room and needed to go.

"Come on, Stelle. What you need your purse for? I'm hungry," my dad said.

"I won't take me but a minute," she said and looked at me. "Walk with me, Simone."

We walked toward the elevator in silence. As soon as we got on, my mom went on a rampage.

"You still haven't told him that dreadful life you led? He seems to be a good man, and you should not keep things from him. Simone, if you don't tell him, I can't promise you that I won't."

She was right. She could not promise that it would not come out.

I had told my mother weeks ago about wanting to tell him, but the time never seemed right.

"The right now is always the right time," she had answered.

She retrieved her purse while I waited in the hall. As we walked back to the elevator, I asked her about the phone call she had received.

"Some woman with a funny accent called the house late this afternoon. She said that we wouldn't be seeing you today because something bad was going to happen to you and Devlin on your way here." She paused. "And you know how I worry about you."

*Trinity*, I thought. In all the years I had known her, I never thought her to be as vindictive as she now appeared.

"Mother, why didn't you just call my cell?" I asked.

"We are your parents and we are concerned. Sometimes, especially when you receive a call like that, as a parent, your initial response is to worry, then common sense sinks in."

Later that night, as Devlin and I were preparing to go to bed, I knew it was time. As my mother said, the right now is always the right time.

"Devlin, do you remember what you said to me the other night?" I began, hoping to postpone the conversation.

"Baby, I'm sorry, but I've said a lot of things to you over the past few days. Can you refresh my memory?"

He stared at me, waiting for a response. Words continued to flow through my mind, but none would come. The only thing that I could think of was how I would feel if his reaction was a negative one. What would I do if he decided to leave me?

*Ring. Ring.*

I knew who it was before I answered.

"Yes, Mother."

"Simone, I know you and Devlin are not sleeping in the same room," she said so loud Devlin heard her.

I hung up.

"So, what is it that I said to you?" he asked, still laughing at me for hanging up on my mother.

"You told me how much you loved me."

"And I do. And I always will," he answered, watching me with those hazel eyes. Those eyes always made me melt. I didn't want to lose the love shining from those eyes. It was those eyes that convinced me to keep my past a secret for another day.

The next two days were pretty much the same as that first evening in Montgomery: spending time with my parents, allowing them to become more acquainted with Devlin and Henry.

On Saturday morning, we went to Tuskegee to visit all of the historic sites. When we returned to the hotel that evening, my mother thought we were all going to sit around and talk with them, but I didn't want to take any chances for her to have a sudden slip of the tongue. Instead, I decided to take Devlin out to Igor's, to listen to live jazz and have a few drinks.

On Sunday my dad insisted we join them for church. I had to admit that it felt wonderful to be back at home and introduce my future husband and father-in-law to my father's church family, after being gone for so long.

After church, the members had prepared a big meal on our behalf. Henry appeared to enjoy himself, and had a few of the widowed women vying for his attention. It was good to see a smile on his face.

Over the months, I had grown to love Henry just as much as I loved Devlin. It was amazing how much Devlin was like his father, especially since they had only been together in the last six months.

"Henry, Sister Cole was all up on you, piling your plate with her potato salad," I said, joking with him on the ride home. "Looks like you may have to take a few trips back down here to visit her."

"Look here, baby girl," he said as he looked back from the driver's seat at me. "That potato salad was good as all outdoors, but that Sister Cole was a li'l bit too old for me."

"Old?" I chimed. "If I'm not mistaken, she is in her mid-fifties. That's younger than you, isn't it?"

"And that's too old for me. Hell, I am old my damn self, so what I need an old woman for? Two old people are just like two dead batteries. Can't get a damn thing started."

We laughed practically all the way back.

The next morning, Charlene came into my office to get details of my visit back home. Devlin was on his way over to take the promo pictures for our upcoming nuptials.

"So, she called your parents' house?" Charlene asked after I told her about my weekend activities.

"It appears that she did."

"So, how did your parents get along with Devlin and his father?" she asked, changing the subject.

I smiled, thinking about my parents' approval of him and how my father and Henry interacted like old friends who had not seen each other in years.

"They loved him and he seemed to love them."

"Cool," she said as she walked out.

A few moments later, I looked up and saw my Darius Lovehall standing at the door.

"What's up, pretty lady?" he asked.

"You," I said as I walked over to him and hugged and kissed him.

# 23
# *Devlin*

My dad called and asked if I would stop by on my way home from the studio. I enjoyed spending time with him.

Once I got to his house, I saw him sitting on the couch crying. In front of him sat a half-empty bottle of whiskey.

"Are you okay, Pop?" I asked, already knowing the obvious.

I noticed something in his hand. It was the letter from Grammy.

"Why did I have to take your mother out to that club?" he asked.

I sat on the couch, wanting to cry too. It hurt me to see him in so much pain.

"She said she didn't want to go. I didn't listen," he cried.

I wanted to tell him that it wasn't his fault, but this demon had lived with him for over thirty years, and my words wouldn't be of comfort to him.

We both sat silently for several moments. It hurt that I was unable to help him. I remembered how I had felt when he revealed his identity. I wanted to hate him. I needed to hate him for not being a part of my life and waiting over thirty years to return to it. I wanted him to feel bad for not being a part of my life. But he had lived his entire life in a shell, and that made me sad for him.

I continued to sit with him, watching him drink straight from the bottle and stare at the letter.

"I'm sorry, son," he finally said.

"You don't have anything to be sorry about."

"Here, read this," he slurred as he handed me the letter.

*December 19, 2004*
*Dearest Henry,*

*I knows you wondering why this letter is coming to you earlier than usual, but this morning when I woke up I didn't feels so good and I just wanted to make sure that you heard from me one last time in case the good Lord called me home. I haven't told Devlin, but for the past year, them doctors tells me that I have a bad heart. I didn't want that boy to worry 'bouts me. He got so much other stuff going on his mind. That boy so smart 'til it don't make no sense.*

*I been praying all these years that you would come to see that boy, spend time with him and let him know how much you loves him. I know you loves him, Henry. Like I always say, I can still remember the look you had in your eyes when you first held him.*

*Now, I don't know how much longer the good Lord gon' give me here on this earth, but I feels like this may be the last one. I called my friend Betty to come over here to mail you this here letter just in case the Lord calls me home today.*

*Henry, all these years you blamed yourself for what happened and you shouldn't. Some days I finds myself blaming me. If I had let Sarah go up North with you when you first asked, maybe she would still be here with us now, but I thought I was doing what was best then.*

*I remembers when we were all at the hospital and you told me that he was aiming at you and that it should've been you. Well no, baby, I don't believe that to be true. God took who He knew was ready to meet Him and that was our Sarah. You done right by us all these years and that's why God left you here.*

*The money you sent, it's sitting in an account and when I'm gone, Devlin will be fine, but that boy going to be all right anyway. He such a smart and caring boy, but he needs all his family. Please come and see about the boy.*

*Well, I'm getting tired now, so I'm going to lie down and read some of God's Word. Think I will put this letter in my Bible and say a prayer before Betty gets here.*

*Love always,*

*Essie Mae Carter*

*P.S. I heard rumors about what happened to that boy who shot our Sarah. I don't know and I don't even care to know if those rumors are true, but from what I hear whatever happened to him, nobody missed him after he left. But I know a lot of people who missed you. Come on home, now. It's time.*

I looked at the date: December 19, 2004. The same day she died. Ms. Betty had found her lying on her bed with her Bible on top of her.

My father took another drink. I read the letter again. What Grammy said about the man who shot my mother bothered me. She wrote that no one missed him after he was gone.

I had asked him what happened, but he always told me that I did not want to know. My curiosity was piqued, but I knew that it was going to take time before he told me more about that night, just like it took him time to come back into my life. But I needed to know why he had waited thirty years to return.

My father drank himself into oblivion. He carried more demons than I could ever have imagined, more demons than any one man should carry alone.

I recalled the week Jacob died. Until the day I met Simone, I had done the exact same thing as my father, searching for peace in a drunken stupor.

I remained at his house for hours, watching him cry, laugh about an old memory, then cry again until he finally passed out. I helped him to his room and laid him on the bed. On my way back downstairs, I called Simone.

"Hey," she said, sounding excited.

"Hey, I'm just calling to let you know that I'm going to stay over here at my dad's tonight."

"Is everything okay?"

"Somewhat. He's just having a hard time right now."

"Poor thing, he really loved your mother," she said somberly.

"Yes, he sure does. He loved her beyond death," I said softly.

My father was up making breakfast at seven o'clock in the morning.

"Want some of this liver mush?" he asked, eating it straight from the package.

"No, thank you. I don't do the mush thing," I said, laughing.

"Outside of missing you, your grammy, and your mother all those years in New Jersey, I think good old liver mush is what I missed the most," he laughed, swallowing the mushy black substance.

"Son," he started as he finished eating his breakfast, "I want to do something special for you and Simone. Like a party or something. We could have it here."

"You don't have to do anything like that," I said. "Just having you around is enough for me."

Tears formed in his eyes. He hugged me.

"That's the best thing I've heard in years, son. I love you. I still want to do something special for you and baby girl. Okay?"

"Yes, sir," I replied, realizing that he would not take no for an answer.

"Good," he said as he walked to the refrigerator. "I can call Robert back now so that he can make preparations for him and Estelle to fly down Thursday evening."

"You've already spoken to them?" I smiled, realizing that we were having an engagement party, whether we wanted it or not.

As I drove home that morning, I thought about our weekend trip to Alabama. I was excited that we all appeared to get along. And I finally understood what Simone had been telling me about her mother. At the same time, I believed that she should see it as a blessing to know her mother and spend time with her.

My home phone was ringing when I walked into the house. I quickly ran to answer it.

"Hello," I said, feeling that it was going to be another hang-up.

"Do you really know the bitch you're marrying?" the voice asked.

"Who is this?"

*Click.*

I placed the phone back on the receiver, perplexed about the call. I did not recognize the voice, but the woman on the other end had an accent. The calls we had been receiving over the past few weeks came to mind. There was only one person I thought it could be, but ever since I told her we were over, I had not heard from her. I assumed that she was finally making things work with Thomas.

"Do you want me to ride with you?" I asked Simone after she informed me that she was going to the airport to pick up her parents.

"No, that's okay, but you are welcome to come over later for dinner," she suggested.

"You know, if we had been thinking, they could have come back with us on Sunday."

"No, that would not have worked out too well." She giggled.

"And why would that not have worked out?"

"Well," she began, still giggling, "My mom can't travel by car for a long period of time. She gets a severe case of diarrhea."

"Does she get the boonts?" I asked, laughing.

"Does she get the what?"

"Never mind, I will tell you about that later." I continued to laugh as we hung up the phone.

I stayed over at my father's house again that night, mostly because he and Simone lived so close to each other that we could all ride to the studio together. I also felt the strong urge to be as close to my father as possible. I worried that his demons would soon completely take over.

Every time he mentioned the night of my mother's death, some more of him died. His pain was still as great as the day it actually happened.

"Son," he said as we both sat on the patio watching the waterfall of his pool.

"Simone is a damn good woman. She's a strong woman." He paused to sip his beer. "Not just because she is successful at what she does, but because she loves strong." He paused again and looked over at me. "Do you know what that means, to love strong?"

I shook my head no.

"When I say that she loves strong, I mean she loves with all she has. It is like a fire burning wood. It burns to the end, until the only thing seen are the ashes."

I still did not understand what he meant, but I listened. Living with Grammy most of my life taught me that sometimes the things older people say seem like they don't make sense, but over time you remember and understand.

# 24
## *Simone*

*Click.*

Trinity and her phone calls had finally taken me over the edge. I had tried calling her to ask her to act like an adult for a change, but the phone would just ring. No voice mail picked up or anything.

"Simone, it's nine o'clock, baby. Don't you think it's time for you to go to bed? I don't want us to be late in the morning," my mother said to me as she walked into my room wearing her nightgown.

"Mom, I am fine. I arrive at work every morning before seven. I've been doing it for years now," I said matter-of-factly.

"Well, tomorrow is a big day."

"Yes, ma'am, it sure is. Why don't you go lie down, okay?" I said as I directed her to the guest room.

After taking a shower, I attempted to call Trinity one more time. There was no answer. I was nervous that she would do something crazy before, during, or after the show the following morning. I hoped that I could do something to defuse the situation.

As I lay in my bed, I thought about the bomb threat we received while taping the show earlier that day.

"I think it will be best to have extra security," Suzette had said. "I would rather be safe than sorry."

"I agree," I said as I nervously paced the parking lot while a bomb squad checked the building.

"Could there be anyone else that would do this?" Charlene asked. "I mean, seriously, was your na-na that damned good to her?" She was trying to make me laugh, but it did not work.

Back inside the studio, I was a nervous wreck. My hands and knees shook constantly.

Suzette walked in with two detectives.

"Your producer told us that you have been receiving harassing phone calls and also received a dead rat. Is that correct?"

"Yes," I said to the tall black detective.

"Did you call the police upon receiving the rodent, ma'am?"

"No, I did not," I responded as I took a deep breath.

"Can I ask why not?" the detective's short, stubby white partner asked as he gave me a look of suspicion.

Suzette noticed my nervousness about discussing the situation.

"Okay, look," she began. "Everything else that is said from this point must be on a need-to-know basis to your department. Is that understood?" she asked with authority.

After they both agreed, she called Charlene to come in. As my publicist, this was her area of expertise.

Before the officers left, they offered to provide me with

security until the matter was contained, but I quickly declined.

"Why the hell did you decline protection, Simone?" Suzette asked, standing up as if she were going to retract my request.

"Suzette, please. I don't want to make something big out of something little," I said, thinking I was making all the sense in the world.

She sat back down and stared at me.

"Look, sugarplum, someone is up to something. It may be just a prank, but what if this thing is serious? Devlin, his father, your parents—all of them could be in danger as well."

I did not say a word. I knew she was right, but I honestly did not think that Trinity would do anything to harm any of us. It was just her way of attempting to make me afraid.

"You need to at least talk to him and let him know what's going on," Suzette said as she walked out the door.

"She's right, you know? You need to tell Devlin everything," Charlene said as she followed Suzette.

I knew that it was time for him to know, but I was still afraid. Afraid of losing the man I loved, afraid of losing my Darius Lovehall.

The next morning, Devlin and Henry were outside waiting on us at six AM. We drove to the studios together with everyone chitchatting, except me.

"Is everything okay?" Devlin asked.

I nodded my head yes, but I knew the truth and realized that he knew something was going on.

Once we arrived, there were several police cars surrounding the studio.

"What's going on here?" my mother asked.

"Extra security," I said as I got out of Henry's SUV.

"Why?" Devlin asked me suspiciously. I continued to walk in the building.

"Come with me to my office."

Once we arrived in my office, I closed the door.

"What's going on, Simone?" Devlin asked again, with more concern than before.

I sat down on the couch and took a deep breath. Devlin sat beside me, then grabbed my hand.

"We had a bomb threat yesterday and Suzette wanted extra security to be on the safe side."

"Why didn't you mention this to me yesterday?" he asked.

I did not have an answer.

"Is there anything else I need to know?" he asked.

I looked in his eyes. Those damn eyes. I suddenly thought about the first time I saw his picture and how it was his eyes that brought me closer. It was his eyes that made me melt. I did not want to lose those eyes.

*Knock, knock, knock.*

My mother walked in uninvited and took a seat in one of the chairs in front of my desk.

"Simone, what in the world is going on here?" she asked.

"Mother, can you please give Devlin and me a few moments alone?" I asked.

"If you think I'm going to leave your side right now, you must be crazy," she answered, refusing to leave.

The show went smoothly and without any disruptions. Immediately after taping, we were interviewed by several reporters from different stations, entertainment shows, and magazines.

"I think I may like this," Henry said of being in the spotlight.

"Well, you can have all of this foolishness," my mother responded.

Henry invited us all to his house to discuss the plans for our upcoming engagement party.

"Henry Carlisle," I began as I pulled Charlene toward his SUV. "This is my publicist, Charlene Humphries. I think she would be a great asset to you while planning something short notice."

Henry gave her a devious look, and then smiled a devious smile. "Baby girl, I can use all the as-s-sets that I can get."

"Henry, you are a mess," I said, laughing.

"Baby girl, that's not all I am. Hello, Ms. Humphries," he said as he grabbed her hand. "Will you be joining us for lunch?" he asked her.

She gave her hand to him and if I did not know any better, she appeared to be blushing.

"Yes, Mr. Carlisle, I will be joining you all for the afternoon."

"Call me Henry," he said seductively.

It was almost ten PM when we finished the planning. My mother had already fallen asleep watching the Lifetime Network in Henry's den. My father and Devlin sat outside by the pool, where they had been talking for most of the afternoon and evening. Several times I saw my dad reach over and pat Devlin on the shoulder, making me curious about their conversation. I was pleased at the connection my father seemed to have with Devlin, but I was still afraid of waiting so long to tell him about my past.

I sat at the dining room table with Henry and Charlene, and it appeared to me that he enjoyed having her around. She seemed to enjoy being around him as well.

"Mr. Carlisle—" He gave her a stern look that she immediately caught. "Henry, your place is beautiful."

"Would you like a tour?" he asked.

As they walked off on the tour, I decided to join my dad and future husband outside on the patio. I thought that I would try to get a little peek at what they had been talking about all day.

"There she is," my dad said as I walked over and sat on his lap. "Honey, Devlin is an upstanding man. We really took some time today to get to know each other," he said as I smiled and kissed my father on the cheek.

When I finally got home, I hopped in the tub and cursed myself out.

"You're a cowardly bitch, Simone. The man loves you, and you love him. Why did you wait so long?"

I recalled the look of concern Devlin gave me when we first entered the studio that morning and he saw the police. When I told him what had happened the day before, he was more concerned about my safety than being angry with me.

The next morning, I woke up feeling sick.

"Must have been something I ate," I said to myself as I walked to the bathroom. But everything that I had eaten the night before spewed out. Clinging to the toilet, I tried to remember what I had eaten that would make my stomach feel this way.

Although I still felt sick, I headed home late that afternoon. I had hoped to spend some time with Devlin, but he was out with both of our fathers the entire day. I went straight to my room, trying my best to avoid my mother.

I created the hottest bath that I could and turned on the motors to the Jacuzzi and lay in the refreshing water. My mind roamed free from everything that was going on. Free from my pain-in-the-ass mother. Free from Trinity's threats. Free from this nauseating pain in my stomach.

I got out of the tub and went straight to bed.

My home phone rang as I began to drift off. I turned the ringer off. I was not in the mood for the hang-ups. My cell phone rang. I answered it.

"Your party is about to end, bitch," the woman with a strange accent said, then hung up.

I sat up in my bed. I called Devlin but only received his voice mail. I looked over at the clock. Ten-fifteen PM. I checked on my mother in the guest room, where she and my dad were asleep. I began to worry. I tried calling Devlin at his house phone, but still got no answer.

I paced my room for a few more moments, and then tried calling Henry.

"Hello," he said cheerfully.

"Hey, Henry, this is Simone. Is Devlin still there?" I asked nervously.

"No, baby girl. He and your dad left here around eight. He said he was heading home after he dropped your father off."

I hung up without saying good-bye. My stomach was in knots thinking about the threatening call I had just received.

I quickly threw on a pair of jeans and a T-shirt, grabbed my purse, and headed to my car. As I drove to Devlin's house, all of my thoughts were on the accented caller.

"Was that Trinity?" I asked myself aloud. "No, it couldn't have been."

# 25

## *Devlin*

"We both tried to protect our daughter the best way we knew how. Her mother can be a bit trying at times, but she loves that child more than anything."

As we sat on my father's patio, I listened to Simone's father as he spoke passionately of his daughter.

"Your father told me about your mother. I'm very sorry that happened," he said softly. "I had the opportunity to talk with him alone while you guys were in Alabama, and I must say that man is what I call a real man." He paused and placed his hand on my shoulder.

"Sometimes a person can love so hard that no matter what comes their way, that love will never break." He paused again and took a sip of his water.

"In my thirty-odd years as a pastor, I've married a lot of people, and I will tell you the truth. The way I see the look in your eyes when you look at my daughter is rare."

"Your daughter is rare, sir," I said softly.

"Yes, that she is." He became quiet as he stared at the pool's waterfall. "I see that same look in her eyes when she looks at you too."

We sat on the patio talking for most of the day. It was a wonderful feeling. After being fatherless for over thirty years, I had gained two fathers in less than one year.

"She can sometimes be stubborn, though. As a girl, she could do anything that she set her mind to do. Her mother wanted her to be a teacher, but she had her eyes set on TV, and she never took her eyes off it."

"Mr. Jackson, Simone entered my life during a time when I felt God had forgotten about me," I said, feeling ashamed. "I had basically given up on God. Period. Simone seemed to have appeared as if she were my angel."

He began to smile.

"She was our angel." He stared up at the sky as if he saw something. "Stelle had lost two babies before Simone, and in both of those deaths, parts of Stelle died. Parts of me died too. When she was born, we both vowed that we would protect her from any and everything, and sometimes I believe we tried to hold on too hard, too scared to let go."

He surprised me with that statement. Simone often told me that her mother constantly nagged her about her life choices.

"Although I never said a word about any of her decisions, deep down I never wanted my baby to leave. Now, I am going to say this, and I will leave it alone. I will not lie and say I agreed with all of her decisions in life, because some hurt me more than any man would ever know, but I knew that they were her decisions to make, and I knew that the more I tried to hold her back, the more she would rebel and fight."

I wanted to know more about his last comment, but decided to leave it alone.

* * *

After hours of idle talk, I felt that I knew more about Simone through the eyes of her father than from any conversation she and I ever had.

But the past few days lingered on my mind—the hang-ups we had received; the distressing call her parents received on our way to Alabama; the bomb threat at the studio she did not tell me about, in addition to the call I received about not knowing the woman I was about to marry.

"Is he out here lying to you, Devlin?" Simone asked as she walked out and sat on her father's lap.

"No, not at all," I said, smiling.

"Now, look here," Reverend Jackson began. "I see and feel love here. I want you both to promise me that no matter what comes your way, you will trust in the love that God has given you." He stood up and left Simone and me alone on the patio.

"I love you, Devlin," she said as she came over to me and sat on my lap.

"I love you too."

She stared at me long and hard as if she had something to say.

"What's wrong?" I asked.

Something about her attitude the past few weeks had me thinking the worst. But just as she was about to say something, we heard the loud sound of her mother's voice.

"Do you not see the time, Robert? That child has a job to go to in the morning."

"Stelle, leave them kids be," Reverend Jackson said, but Mrs. Jackson did not listen.

"Simone, honey, it's getting late, and you know you have to be at work in the morning." She walked over to me, and to my surprise, kissed me on my cheek. "You stay sweet, Devlin, and we will see you tomorrow."

As we watched Simone, her parents, and Charlene drive away, I noticed my dad had taken a special interest in Charlene.

"So, is that your age range?" I asked jokingly.

"Son, I like them young, but not that young. I ain't trying to have a heart attack." He laughed. "It's just good to know that my eyes can still see, and my Johnson can still rise."

I laughed at my father's comment. It was amazing how he still found humor, despite all of his pain. It was something I had never been able to do.

I stayed at his place again. It had become my third home over the past few weeks.

The next morning, my father, Reverend Jackson, and I decided to spend the day together just hanging out. I enjoyed being around the two old and wise men, and they truly enjoyed being around each other, which pleased me.

They acted as if they were old friends that had known each other for many years and had recently rekindled their friendship. It was a good feeling to know that I would finally be a part of a real family.

While we ate lunch, my phone rang.

"Today, you will know about the woman you plan to marry," the same voice from the day before said.

"Who is this?" I asked angrily.

*Click.*

"Is everything all right, son?" my father asked.

"Dad, to be honest, I really don't know what's going on," I said as I pressed the off button on my phone.

I took Reverend Jackson back to Simone's house, and my father back to his place. Then I drove home thinking about Simone and looking forward to spending the rest of my life with the angel that God allowed to enter my life.

As I pulled in my driveway, I noticed a yellow manila envelope stuck in my door.

*Mr. Devlin Carter*

I was not expecting anything. My curiosity went into overdrive. Inside the package was a typed noted attached to a plain-cover DVD.

*As promised, this is the day you really know the bitch you are planning to marry!*

*T.*

"Who the hell is T?" I asked myself aloud.

I immediately put the disc into my DVD player. The first person I saw was Simone lying on a bed, naked. Suddenly, another naked body joined her. The video held my undivided attention when I saw the second woman, the color of honey, walk over to her. As Simone lifted her legs open, the woman began to taste her sweetness. My heart dropped. I pressed the off button on the remote.

"It couldn't have been her," I said as I pressed the play button again and continued to watch. My eyes remained glued to the screen until Simone screamed in pleasure the same way she screamed her joys of pleasure with me.

A sudden and hard pain hit my heart deeper than any pain I had ever felt. It all made sense. The phone calls. The bomb threat. Her strange attitudes and, most importantly, her father's comments to me earlier that evening.

"I won't lie and say I agreed with all of her decisions in life," he had said, "because some hurt me more than any man would ever know."

I played the video repeatedly, hoping and wishing that it was not the woman I loved. Hoping and wishing that I would soon awake from the nightmare. But every time I watched, I saw the same two people. One was Simone, the other was T.

My phone rang constantly, but I did not answer. I could not talk. I did not want to talk.

"She could have told me before I fell in!" I yelled.

The pain felt devastating, and the only thing I knew to do in pain was to drink.

I went to the pantry and pulled out the bottle of Crown Royal. As I went back to the living room, I guzzled directly from the bottle. It burned my throat, something that had not happened in years, but I did not care. I needed to drink until I reached a state of oblivion.

I placed the bottle on the coffee table, rewound the disc, played it again, rewound it again, and played it again.

*Knock, knock, knock.*

"Who the hell is it?" I yelled.

"Devlin, it's me, Simone."

"What the fuck do you want?" I screamed.

"Baby, are you okay?"

"Go back to where you came from."

"Devlin, baby, what's wrong? I'm coming in," she said. I heard her place the key I had given her into the keyhole.

She lingered at the door. I did not look at her, but I could feel her eyes piercing me.

"Devlin, baby, what's wrong?" she asked. Her voice trembled.

I remained silent, then pressed the play button on the DVD. I turned my eyes toward her to see her reaction. Tears fell from her eyes.

"Devlin," she said softly, "I can explain."

"Explain?" I asked angrily. "Explain that I am engaged to a lesbian and I am just finding out?"

"I'm not a lesbian," she whispered.

"Oh, excuse me, a bisexual?"

"I'm not bisexual either," she said.

"Not a lesbian and not a bisexual. So are you telling me that what I see right here is you with a man that looks like a woman?"

She sat down in the chair closest to the door, with her head down.

"Devlin, will you please listen?" she asked.

I hit the replay button again.

"Before you, I lived an alternative lifestyle. But it was never what I really wanted."

The video ended, and I started it over again.

"You are my dream. Please don't wake me up."

Again, I rewound and replayed the video.

"Devlin, are you listening to me? I love you. Not her, not any woman or any other man," she said, crying. "I love you."

I looked over at her and I felt nothing. All the love I had for her had suddenly disappeared. All that was left, all that I saw, was the shell of an illusion. This was something she should have mentioned to me when we met.

"Simone," I began, trying to remain calm, "oddly enough, I am not mad about your past. I am pissed off at how I found out. All these months I have confided my entire fucking life to you, and you chose not to tell me this. Can you tell me why not?"

As she shook her head no, I stood from my couch.

"I need to be alone," I said, directing her to leave.

She looked up at me in total disbelief. She remained seated, not wanting to leave.

"Can we please talk?" she asked.

"We had over seven months to talk about this situation, so just as you chose to wait, I'm going to choose to wait too and discuss this when I am damn good and ready."

After my last comment, she emerged from the chair and walked out of the door, but remained on the porch. I walked outside with her.

We both stood on the porch in silence. I happened to notice an older model Chevy Caprice parked across the street with its parking lights turned on. As soon as we walked outside to the porch, the car drove slowly away.

"I tried telling you several times, Devlin, I really did," she began as if she refused to wait and discuss this. "Something always seemed to come up every time. Please don't allow this to destroy us."

I felt my heart soften again. In the past several months, my own life situations, past and present, had saturated our relationship. Maybe I was to blame for her not saying anything sooner; however, I was still hurt. The way it came to my attention was cruel, although I knew it was not her doing.

"Who's T?" I asked as I noticed the same car drive by slowly a third time. "That was the name on the note that the disc came with."

"Her name is Trinity," she said softly.

"We will talk tomorrow, okay?" I asked, finally feeling my love for her return.

"Okay," she said softly.

As she began to walk to her SUV, the Chevy Caprice stopped directly in front of my house. The driver's side window lowered and a shiny object poked its face out the window, aiming at Simone.

*Pow!*

I have no idea what overtook me, but the only thing that came to mind was the comment my father once made about the night of my mother's death.

*Son, I wish I could go back twenty-five seconds before it happened.*

# 26

## *Simone*

My heart was beating fast and my head felt as if a hundred bricks had struck me. The police asked numerous questions. Questions I really did not have any answers to.

"Did you see what type of car it was?" the officer asked. "Did you see the shooter?"

My only answer was that I did not know.

After Devlin told me he needed to be alone and promised we would talk the following day, I walked to my car. The last thing I heard was what sounded like thunder and Devlin calling my name. When I turned to face him, his body hovered in the air and then blanketed me as we both fell to the ground. There was a loud crash followed by shattered glass and the squeal of spinning tires. Devlin's body fell limp as he slid to the side of me.

"Devlin, are you okay?" I asked, but got no answer. I tapped his shoulder. He did not move. I continued to call his name. He did not respond. My entire body shook uncontrollably.

Several of his neighbors came to their doors as I yelled for someone to call for help. I held him in my arms, crying, wishing he would wake up; however, he lay there with his eyes closed and blood pouring from his arm.

When we arrived at the hospital, it seemed as if the entire world knew what happened. Reporters were everywhere.

"Ms. Jackson, can you tell us what happened?" one reporter said as she stuck her microphone in my face. I shoved it back in her direction. I did not want to talk to anyone. I wanted to be with Devlin, to make sure he was okay.

The EMT workers carried Devlin into an area marked PERSONNEL ONLY, but I refused to leave his side.

"Ma'am, can you please step back?" the nurse asked. I do not remember what I said to her, but I remember the look she gave me before she left me alone.

As I stood there watching them wheel Devlin away, I kept my eyes in their direction, never blinking.

"Ms. Jackson, I know that this is a difficult time right now, but please, can you tell me anything that you may be able to remember?" the officer asked again.

As I sat in the hard chair, my eyes filled with tears. I had no answers. I had no words that could help them.

"Let's give her a few moments," I heard the officer's partner say.

I placed my feet up on the chair, wrapped my arms around my legs and laid my head on my knees, mentally beating myself up. Over and over again I told myself that I had caused what had happened.

I got up from the chair and asked the nurse if I could see him. She told me the same thing that she had told me the last ten times I asked.

"Ma'am, someone will come out as soon as they can to give you an update," she said in an aggravated tone.

I wanted to call her a bitch and make her go back there and get someone. I wanted to grab what little bit of hair she had and force her to obey my command.

"Look, that's my fiancé in there. I really could do without your attitude," I said. She looked at me as if she couldn't care less.

"Ms. Jackson, believe me; I understand your concern, but there is nothing you can do at this point but wait."

I stared at her. I had many names I wanted to call her. I thought about knocking the shit out of her, but she was not my enemy. She had done nothing wrong.

As I walked back over to the chair I was sitting in, my parents, Henry, and Suzette approached with looks of concern.

"Simone, baby, are you okay?" my mother was the first to ask. She embraced me and my entire body became a hot volcano. I vomited all over her.

"Ms. Jackson, can I get you anything?" the nurse asked.

"I'm fine," I said uncertainly.

My father helped me back into the chair and I looked over at my mother and tried to apologize, but she was not bothered by my vomit on her.

"What happened? Is that blood on your clothes yours? Where is Devlin?" My mom rattled off each question without waiting for an answer to any of them.

As I looked up to answer, I noticed that Charlene had joined us.

"They are sending us to a private section of the hospital," she said.

We arrived at the private waiting room. I noticed Henry sat alone in the far corner, away from everyone and away from me, the woman who caused his son to be here.

I wanted to go to him and console him, but I was in no shape to do that. I knew that he thought it was my fault, and that we were all there because of my actions. It was my fault that after he had waited so long to be with his son, I was the reason that he might lose Devlin again.

I explained everything I could remember. I looked back over at Henry again. Our eyes met. We were kindred souls meeting for the first time. One tear tumbled down his face. He got up from his chair and walked over to me.

"Can we talk?" he asked me.

"Henry, I'm very sorry for what just happened to Devlin, and you know I am concerned and hope nothing but the best for him, but Simone is in no shape to talk right now. She needs her rest," my mother said, but I did not listen to her.

As I stood up, my mother grabbed me by the arm.

"Simone, you need to re—"

"Stelle, let the girl go," my father demanded.

"Robert, I will do no such thing. For all we know that fool person that did that to Devlin could be right here in this hos—"

"Stelle, I said let her go." His voice became louder as he walked toward her.

"Robert, I will not let—"

"*Estelle Jackson.* For just once in your life, *will you just shut the hell up?*"

My father's voice shook the entire room. I had never heard my father talk to anyone that way, much less my mother. I was startled, and from the look on my mother's face, I could tell that she was too.

"I am not one to lay blame," he began as I slowly walked away toward Henry. "But I hold you responsible for all that's going on right now, and I lay blame on me for not stopping you a long time ago. All those years of demanding so much from our only child. You pushed her away, and I be *damned* if I'm going to let you do it again. So for me, and for everyone in here, just *shut up.*"

* * *

The entire floor was empty, so Henry and I took a walk down the long hallway.

I was nervous. I did not know what to say or how to say it. But I felt guilty. Guilty because I knew with all my heart that I was the cause of this. Guilty because I knew I could have prevented all of this.

We walked in silence for several moments before either one of us said anything. We stopped when we came to a section where a large window overlooked the front entrance of the hospital.

"So, is this the price of fame?" Henry asked as he pointed to all the news crews standing outside to get the big story.

I slowly nodded my head. I had caused this man, who had nothing but tragedy in his life, to have suffered more.

"Henry," I said, trying not to cry, "I'm sorry."

"Sorry for loving my son?" he asked. "Baby girl, there is nothing to be sorry about." He continued to stare out the window.

"The person that shot Devlin was shooting at me," I whispered. "A former lover that I was involved with in the past, a woman," I said, looking at him to see what his reaction would be.

Tears fell from his eyes, causing more tears and emotions to emerge from me.

"He protected you," Henry whispered.

We both continued to stare out of the window, watching the madness below. The madness down there could not match the madness we were all feeling in our hearts.

"This reminds me of January fifteenth, 1974," he began softly. "I asked Sarah to marry me. Devlin was two at the time." He paused and smiled as if that day was a day that he thought of often. "She wanted to stay in, but I had to insist that we go to that club." He paused again. "That damned club was the last time I saw Sarah alive. Devlin's grandmother tried to get me to stay at the hospital that night, but after they pronounced my Sarah dead, I had some business to take care of."

My emotions were uncontrollable. I cried as he spoke.

"After asking a few people if they had seen the guy that shot her, I got word that he was back at the same club, smoking a joint in the back of the building." He took a deep breath.

"Simone, what I'm about to tell you, I have never shared this with anyone in my life, but I believe that once I tell you this, you will understand that I know what's going on inside of you right now." He paused again as if he was remembering something that he longed to forget.

"When Spanky looked up and saw me coming toward him, he pulled out that same damned gun that he used to shoot Sarah and aimed it at me, but there was so much anger in me, so much rage, that I didn't feel fear. He pulled the trigger but missed me. The bullet passed right by me and I kept walking. Once I reached him, he tried to apologize, but I didn't hear him." He wiped his tears with his hands. "I punched his ass so hard he fell to the ground crying like the bitch that he was. Before I knew anything, I had wrapped my hands around his throat until all signs of life were no more."

"And that's why you left," I whispered.

"I didn't want my son to be raised by someone who had committed murder."

Once Henry and I returned to the waiting room, Stephanie, Li'l J, Cody, and even Trevor had shown up. After speaking to them and hugging them, I took a seat alone, away from everyone else.

Talking with Henry helped settle my nerves, but I still felt that I could have prevented the entire situation if I had been up front in the beginning. But I did not do what I should have, or could have done.

Several questions played in my head:

*When did Trinity make a tape of us? She knew that I had always been against that. She knew I would never have allowed that. How did she know where Devlin stayed? If Devlin was so angry with me, why did he protect me?*

"Ms. Jackson, can I please have a moment of your time?" said the black detective who came to my office after the bomb threat.

"Sure," I sighed.

"Do you know this woman?"

He showed me a picture of Trinity.

"Yes, that's Trinity Waters, the individual whom we spoke of the other day," I said.

"Can you come down with us for a moment, please?"

My mouth trembled.

"Come down where?" I asked, weary of going anywhere.

"Downstairs," he said.

My stomach turned. Why did I need to go down there?

"Devlin is down in the morgue?" I cried aloud. Everyone rushed over to us.

The detective did his best to calm me down, as well as those around us, but after hours of waiting, we were all on the edge.

"No, ma'am, he is not down there." He paused and looked around at everyone. "But I really need for you to identify the body of the lady you say to be Trinity Waters."

# 27

## *Devlin*

When I woke up, I looked around. Nothing was familiar to me. I was lying on a quilt and wearing black silk pajamas.

The sky was as blue as I had ever seen it, and the grass was a color of green my eyes had never before seen. Mere words could not describe this place. It was beyond any beauty I had ever seen.

I rose up, sat Indian-style on the quilt, and looked around. I didn't feel hot or cold. It was perfect.

I searched for others, but there was no one. I was alone.

"Hello," I said, hearing my voice echo. "Is anyone there?"

A small pond appeared out of nowhere, and a little girl played on its bank.

"Hello," I said, but she didn't respond. She did not even look my way.

"Little girl, are you alone?" I asked. "Where are your parents?"

Still, no words came from her mouth.

I watched her play for what seemed like hours. She didn't have a fear in the world. An overwhelming peace invaded my body. A peace that told me that I could stay there forever and be happy.

"Are we in heaven?" I asked the little girl, but still no words came from her mouth.

I watched her. She was the most beautiful little girl I had laid eyes on. From a distance she looked familiar to me, but I wanted to see her up close. I walked over to her.

It felt as if I had walked for hours to get to her, yet she was only a few feet away. I never reached her. I felt a sudden overwhelming urge to sleep. I turned around to go back to the quilt, but it was right under my feet. I realized that I had not moved an inch.

"I must be in heaven," I said as I smiled and lay back down and fell asleep.

"Black man. Yo, black man, wake up." The familiar voice forced me out of my deep sleep.

When I opened my eyes, I could not believe it. It was Jacob. He wore the same pajamas that I did, only his were the color of pearl.

I looked at him in total disbelief. It wasn't the weak and sickly Jacob that I had watched deteriorate into a shell of his former self. Instead, Jacob looked like he had before his illness had invaded him and stole his life.

"Good to see you, brother." His voice carried the same echo as mine.

"Good to see you as well," I replied. We embraced once he sat on the quilt beside me.

We sat in silence, both watching the little girl play by the pond.

"Who is she?" I asked, but he did not answer.

"Why are you still here?" he asked.

"What do you mean?" I asked.

"It's time for you to go back."

"Go back where?" I asked.

"To where your father is, to where Simone is, back to your family, back to our family."

"You know about my father and Simone?" I asked.

"I can see a lot from up here," he said, smiling.

"So, if you can see a lot, then you know what went down, right?" I asked.

He nodded his head, then gave a slight smile.

"Sometimes, what we think we see is not always what we see. It's rare that our eyes and our minds are able to see the same thing at the same time."

"She lied to me, Jacob," I said.

"No, she didn't lie to you. She just didn't tell you."

"I told her everything."

"And she saw how everything in your life was so overwhelming for you that she was afraid of how you would react to what was going on her life."

There was silence between us. We continued to sit and watch the little girl play by the pond.

"Who is she?" I asked again.

"I have to go now, and so do you."

"Where are you going, Jacob?" I asked, but he did not respond.

He walked away. As he walked by the little girl at the pond, she looked up at him and smiled. She grabbed his hand, pulled Jacob down toward her, and gave him a hug.

The little girl whispered something in Jacob's ear and they both looked in my direction. He smiled and stood straight up. I continued to watch him until he suddenly disappeared.

The little girl remained at the pond alone, playing as I drifted back to sleep.

# 28

# *Simone*

"We received several reports that a gunshot was heard on the top deck of a parking lot in uptown Charlotte. When officers arrived at the scene, they found her laying there with a single close-shot wound to the head," the detective told me as he replaced the white sheet over Trinity's body.

"Do they know who shot her?" I asked.

"It appears to have been suicide. There was no evidence of foul play." He paused as we began to walk out of the morgue. "Some of Mr. Carter's neighbors reported seeing a 1984 Chevy Caprice fleeing the scene. The car Ms. Waters was found laying beside fits that same description."

"She attempted to kill me first?" I asked.

"Ms. Jackson, that's the way it appears."

Two uniformed officers escorted me back to the waiting room. I saw my parents and Henry talking to someone who appeared to be the doctor. I ran over to see if there was any news.

"Ms. Jackson? Dr. Itu," the Asian doctor said as he extended his hand. "I was just informing your family here that your fiancé suffered a subdural hematoma. He's currently in a coma, but he is in stable condition."

My knees became weak when I heard the word *coma.*

"How long will he be in a coma?" I asked nervously.

"It's kind of hard to say. He could be out of it in the next few moments, or in the next few years. There is no definite answer," he said with no emotion.

"When can I see him?"

"Once he comes out of surgery, I will have an orderly come down to inform you."

"Surgery!" I yelled.

"Yes, ma'am. We had to remove the bullet."

"He was shot in the head?" I asked.

I suddenly thought about Trinity's body lying in the morgue. It frightened me to think that Devlin could soon join her.

"No, ma'am. Surprisingly enough, the bullet lodged into his right arm, and touched no major arteries, and he only suffered some minor scratches to his forehead from glass cuts. It was the impact that he sustained from hitting the window that placed him in his current state."

I remembered the shattered glass before he landed on me. It had come from my car when Devlin's head hit it as he shoved me out of the way, taking a bullet that was coming for me. I walked back over to the corner and sat down, remembering my earlier conversation with Henry. Devlin had sacrificed his own life to save mine.

I couldn't believe that Trinity killed herself. I had seen her body with the shot in her head with my own eyes, but I still found it difficult to believe that she would have done that. Trinity was always a strong-willed and strong-minded person. Committing suicide was just too out of character. But the detective had said there were no other traces of foul play.

For months, all of the hang-ups and threats—even the dead rat—was out of character from the Trinity I thought I knew. I realized that I never knew Trinity at all. I realized I never even tried to get to know her.

I had experienced unparalleled happiness with Devlin over the past several months. It was a new feeling, one I had never experienced before. Our relationship had become the most important thing in my life, and now, because of my months of deceit to the man I loved, he could be dying. My thoughts turned to frustration.

"Damn her . . . damn her . . . damn that bitch!" I yelled.

I jumped from my chair, swinging my arms around like a maniac. I was mad. I did not care that she was already dead. I wanted to kill Trinity. I wanted to see her face as I choked the life out of her. I wanted to see the look in her eyes when she knew that I could never love her the way she wanted me to; I could never love her the way I loved Devlin. I wanted to see the look in her eyes when she knew that her last breath was coming and I was the reason it had come.

"Simone." Charlene called my name, trying to calm me down, but I did not hear her.

"Simone." This time it was my mother, but I still refused to respond.

I continued to punch the air, wishing it were Trinity that I was hitting. I was glad that she was dead. I was happy that she was no longer in my life, but I was also sad. Sad because now I knew that I might also be without Devlin.

I finally calmed down, falling into my seat. No one came over to me. No one attempted to give comfort. I placed my feet in the chair and sat in the fetal position, thinking about the last several hours of my life. Finally, I fell asleep.

* * *

"Simone, baby, here, you need to eat something," my mother said, waking me up and handing me a breakfast burrito.

The strong smell of eggs, onions, and cheese triggered something in me. I ran to the nearest trash can, and, as I had done over the past couple of days, vomited.

"Simone, are you okay?" my mother asked with concern.

I could not answer. I did not know myself.

I looked at the clock. It was seven in the morning. We had been there over seven hours, and still no one came out to give us any information. My stomach began to knot again, and it wanted to erupt, but it had been over twelve hours since my last meal, and I had vomited out everything I had in me hours ago.

"Maybe you need to see a doctor," my mother suggested.

"I only want to see Devlin."

"I understand, dear, but you don't look well," my mother said as she placed her arms around me. I accepted her hug, and surprisingly enough, it felt warm.

"Mama," I whispered, "I'm sorry."

"Shh, I'm the one that's sorry," she said as I noticed the tears streaming down her face. I remained in my mother's arms, where I eventually drifted back to sleep.

It was ten AM and we still had not heard anything. I was already on edge, and this waiting made me feel as if I were going to lose my mind.

"Simone," Henry said, walking toward my mother and me. "Why don't you and your mother go home and take a long, hot bath, relax a little. Come back later this afternoon to relieve me and your father."

"Sounds like a plan to me," Charlene said. "I will drive."

I did not want to leave. I wanted to be there when Devlin opened his eyes, but they were right. I needed a break from the hospital.

As soon as we gathered our belongings, an orderly walked in.

"Mr. Carlisle? Ms. Jackson?" he called as he stood at the door.

Henry and I both walked quickly toward him.

"You two are welcome to visit Mr. Carter now. He's in room six-fifty-two," he said, then walked off.

I did not move. I had been waiting to hear those words for the past ten hours. When I finally heard them, I froze. I was afraid.

"Baby girl, go on home now and take that bath," Henry said to me. "You can see him when you get back."

Charlene drove my mother and me to my place. She promised to return in two hours for the ride back to the hospital. She had already arranged for a tow service to pick up my SUV from Devlin's house, and it was at the dealership undergoing repairs from the damages.

"Simone," my mother began once we entered the house, "I want you to know that I meant what I said at the hospital. I'm sorry for all of those years I refused to speak with you and ridiculed you." Tears poured down her face. "I pushed you so hard in your life, thinking I was teaching you, when in all reality I never taught you a thing.

"A couple of weeks ago I was invited to one of my old students' graduation from medical school. She went on and on as to how I was more of a mother to her than her own was mother was. Although that was flattering, I found myself crying inside, wondering why I couldn't have been more of a mother to my own daughter."

"Thank you," I said as I hugged her.

"No, baby, thank you."

* * *

When we arrived back at the hospital, Charlene and my mother returned to the waiting room while I went to see Devlin.

I was scared, unsure of how I would react to seeing him. Henry turned around when he heard me walk in, and moved from the seat beside Devlin's bed.

As I got closer, I noticed Devlin had a smile on his face.

"He's smiling," I said.

"For the past couple of hours, he's been smiling and shedding tears."

"Tears?" I asked.

Henry gave a weird smile, hugged me, and kissed me on my forehead, then left me in the room alone.

I sat and watched him. A lone tear fell from his closed left eye, causing me to cry more.

I thought about Henry's undying love for Devlin's mother. I understood how he felt. I knew I could never love anyone the way I loved Devlin.

# 29

## *Devlin*

When my eyes finally opened again, I was still in the same place, still lying on the same quilt. I looked over at the pond and the little girl was gone. I felt alone again.

I thought about my conversation with Jacob. He had told me I had to go back to my family, but I did not want to go back. I wanted to stay where I was at peace. It was pure silence here. Silence from everything that caused me harm before. There was no one here to lie to me. There was no one here to hurt me. I could not imagine wanting to leave. I dozed off again.

When I opened my eyes, I saw the little girl again.

"Hello," I said.

She still did not respond. She still would not look my way.

I continued to watch her play near the pond alone. I saw someone from a distance walking toward me. As the person got closer, I recognized her.

"Is that you, Grammy?"

Before I received an answer, she was sitting beside me on the quilt.

"Hey, baby. What you doing here?" she asked.

"I'm here to be with you."

She gave a smile and looked at me long and hard, reminding me of the times when I was a child and I did something wrong.

"It's not time for you to be here yet, and you know it," she said.

"Yes, Grammy, it is my time. I want to stay here with you and with Jacob."

"It's not time, Devlin," she said sternly.

"But, Grammy, I don't want to go back. It's nothing but hell for me there."

"Baby, you know betteren anybody that your time is not yet here. You have too much more life to live," she said, then became quiet. "You gots a full life to live. You gots people there depending on you so that they can live. You gots to go back."

"I don't want to. I miss you. I want to stay here with you, here in heaven," I said.

"Baby, this ain't heaven." She smiled at me again, kissed me on my forehead, and held me in her arms. "Simone loves you, baby," she said.

"I love you, Grammy," I said.

"Henry needs you, Devlin."

"I need you," I responded.

"Baby, it's just not your time. You have a lot more work to do. You have a lot of people counting on you right now as we speak. They need you to be back with them."

Tears fell down my face and I felt an overwhelming sadness. I wanted to stay, but somehow I knew I couldn't.

"It's hard, Grammy," I said, trying to make her understand I did not want to leave her.

"It's going to get better, Devlin."

She embraced me, held me long, and began to sing. I fell asleep in her arms.

When I opened my eyes again, she was no longer holding me. She was over by the pond playing and talking with the little girl.

I watched how they interacted with one another. It was beautiful. It was poetic. I stood up from the quilt as I had previously done to walk over to them, but just as before, I never got close to the pond. I was walking, but I remained quiet.

Grammy looked up at me and noticed that I was trying to get to them and before I knew it, she was right back with me.

"The longer you stay here, baby, the longer it will take for you to move. You gots to go back."

We both sat back on the quilt in silence watching the little girl.

"Who's that little girl?" I asked, breaking our silence.

"Baby, you gots to go back home," she said as she stood up.

"Where're you going? Don't go. Stay with me."

She kissed me on my cheek, told me that she loved me, and walked away singing.

*I don't feel no ways tired, Lord.*
*I come too far from where I started from.*
*Nobody told me that the road would be easy.*
*I don't believe he brought me this far*
*To leave me.*

She disappeared, the same way Jacob had done earlier. The little girl remained at the pond playing alone, never acknowledging my existence.

I remained on the quilt, unable to move any farther than where I was. I dozed off.

# 30

## *Simone*

I sat by his side for the remainder of the day, never taking my eyes off him. It was strange to see him smile, but it was even stranger to see the tears fall from his closed eyes.

I heard someone walk in, but I did not bother to look back to see who it was. I refused to take my eyes off him. As I looked at the bandages that surrounded his head and all the scratches on his face, my heart pained.

"This is my fault," I whispered.

"You can't beat yourself up," the voice said from behind me.

When I looked back, I noticed that it was Jacob's wife, Stephanie.

She placed her hand on my shoulder.

"He loves you, Simone."

"I love him," I whispered.

"I had a dream the other night that I didn't understand until now." She paused and walked to the other side of the bed where another chair sat. "I dreamed that Jacob was lying beside me telling me something, but I couldn't really understand what he was saying. Early this morning when I got the call from Henry telling me that you and Devlin were rushed to the hospital, my initial reaction was to panic, but in a matter of seconds I felt a strong peace. I quickly understood what Jacob was saying to me in that dream." She became quiet.

"What did he say?" I asked.

"It's only a storm, baby. It won't last long," she said as I noticed tears falling from her face.

Stephanie and I sat and talked for hours. She told me stories of Devlin and Jacob in college. She gave me more insight on the man I love, on the man who risked his life to save mine.

"I should have told him about my past in the beginning," I said during one of our moments of silence.

"You not telling him would not have changed what happened," she said.

I remained with Devlin until the following morning. I refused to leave his side. Nothing else was important to me. As I drifted off to sleep, Charlene walked in.

"How are you holding up?" she asked.

"Right now, I'm just holding."

"I just finished talking with Detective Green," she began. "The ballistic report on the bullet that shot Devlin came back as a positive match from the same gun that Trinity used to shoot herself."

I did not respond. I continued to sit and watch Devlin.

"After this is over, I need to take some time off. Indefinitely," I said. I was beginning to feel all the pressures of the world fall on my shoulders. I knew that once the press got hold of this story, they would not only harass me, but Devlin as well, and I just could not put him through more pain.

"Simone, this wasn't your fault."

"You told me to tell him, but I didn't," I said.

"That has nothing to do with that crazy bitch shooting him."

"But she was trying to shoot me. I did not take her threats seriously. If I had, then none of this would have happened," I said.

She walked over to me and hugged me. I noticed that her eyes were swollen and full of tears. I had never seen Charlene full of so much sad emotion. She always appeared to be solid as a rock.

"Do you remember the other day what I told you about me being jealous?"

I shook my head yes.

"Tell me this: How many men do you honestly think will step in front of a gun to protect someone they don't love? It's every little girl's dream to have what you and Devlin have. We grow up reading fairy tales of the knight in shining armor." She paused and got some tissue from the small bathroom. When she came back, she kneeled down to me.

"Mr. Carlisle told me about what happened to Devlin's mother."

I knew what she was telling me, without any more words needing to be said. We sat in silence, my eyes focused completely on Devlin. Every now and then Charlene would say something, but I did not really pay any attention to her. All of my attention was on the man that I loved, the man that I might lose.

"Hey, I'm going to get something to eat. Bring you something back?" she asked as she was about to head out of the door.

I shook my head no.

As I sat in the room alone with Devlin, I wondered whether he would be forever gone from my life. Even when he woke up he might not love me any longer. Maybe he would no longer care for me. I cried.

Henry walked in, saw me crying, and suggested that I take a short walk with him to get some air. One of the officers walked with us outside in a private area of the hospital, far away from reporters who were hoping to get their big break.

As we stood outside, allowing a cool summer morning breeze to blow through our torn emotions, I thought about Trinity lying in the morgue.

I had no feeling when I saw her. Looking at her was almost as if I were looking at a complete stranger. I could not even hate her, because to hate, I knew love had to be somewhere in the equation, but it was not.

"Don't spend your years the way I did," he said to me. "Thirty years of regret and inner turmoil. I do not want you to go through that. You do not have to go through that. You are strong and I want you to know, regardless of what happens, we need to be there for each other." He embraced me like a father would his daughter.

Before going back to Devlin's room, I stopped in the waiting room to see my parents.

"Simone, you look terrible," my mother said as she embraced me. "Have you eaten anything yet?"

I shook my head no and sat down. Trevor was in the same corner where I had sat earlier, and he looked as if he could no longer take it.

When he noticed me watching him, he stood up and headed out the door. Li'l J walked behind him. A few moments later, I noticed Li'l J pulling him back into the waiting room as if he were leading him back in, making sure he would never get lost.

I went back to Devlin's room to see if anything had changed. As soon as I stood up, my entire body felt weak.

I had to struggle to stay balanced. The last thing I remembered was lying in Trevor's arms.

"Are you okay?" he asked with sheer concern.

"Thanks. I'm not feeling too well," were the last words I remembered saying. I awoke in my own hospital room.

"What happened?" I asked my mother, who was standing over me.

"You passed out," she said softly.

"Has Devlin awakened yet?"

"Here Simone, eat something," she said as she smiled and tried to force me to eat some form of sandwich she had in her hand.

I quickly pushed it away. I did not want to eat. I wanted to see Devlin. When I tried to get out of bed, my mother refused to let me go until I ate something.

As she watched me eat, the strange smile on her face lingered. It was a look that I had never seen before.

I tried to get out of the bed, but she stopped me again.

"Mother, I have to go see Devlin."

"Not yet," she said. "The doctor is on his way back shortly."

I looked around. She and I were the only ones in the room.

"Why is he coming in here and not Devlin's room?"

She did not answer. She just sat there watching me with that strange smile.

# 31
# Devlin

When I opened my eyes again, I suddenly realized that this time I was not sitting on the quilt near the pond. I was in the pond.

I found myself struggling in the water, feeling as if I were drowning. I felt myself give up and began to sink, until I felt a small hand reach inside and pull me up. When I got to the bank of the pond, I found myself back on the quilt, and the little girl was standing above me.

"Did you pull me up?" I asked, but received no response.

I noticed her features. She was a beautiful, medium brown–complexioned little girl with almond-shaped eyes.

"Where are your parents?" I asked. She returned to the banks of the pond where she continued to play.

I continued to watch her until sleep invaded my body once again.

"Devlin . . . Devlin . . . Wake up, baby."

When I opened my eyes, it took a few moments for my mind to register who was before me.

"Mama?" I asked. She was the exact image of the picture I remembered my father showing me.

"Yes, it's me," she said with a huge smile. "It's good to see you."

I could not speak. There were so many things to say, but all I could do was look long and hard at her through my tears.

"Whe—whe—where did you come from?" I asked nervously.

"I've always been here, within you," she said as she placed her hand on my chest near my heart.

"Always?" I asked.

"Yes, and I will always be with you."

"I've missed you, yet I don't remember you," I said, feeling sad.

"You've done so much, achieved so much. I'm proud of you, Punkin'."

She called me Punkin'. Somehow, I remembered that.

"You know you can't stay, right?"

"Mama, I have to stay. Can I please stay here with you?" I begged.

She shook her head no and smiled. We both sat, staring each other in the eyes. We were two souls who had longed to be together. Two souls that never got the chance to know each other, yet we knew each other well.

"Henry can't take another loss. Not so soon after reclaiming his life," she said.

"He still loves you. I love you."

"I know, but now you two need to move on. You are both standing still," she said as she rubbed her soft hands across my face.

"I don't want to go back. There is nothing left for me," I continued to plead.

"You have a lot left for you there."

"I want to stay here with you. I want to get to know you," I begged.

"You already know me, Devlin. A part of me is in you." She paused and stood up.

"Come walk with me," she said as she reached her hand out to me.

As I held her hand, I felt the love I had always craved. I felt the love that I thought I would never know, a love that a mother has for her child.

We walked in silence and passed familiar places from my life. I saw the elementary school that I attended. The church Grammy took me to every Sunday, the same church where I was baptized at the age of ten. We walked past Jacob's and Trevor's house with the makeshift tree house in the backyard that we had made from some old wood their father had lying around the yard.

"You were here with me all these times?" I asked, breaking the silence.

She only nodded her head as we continued our journey.

Once we came to the end, sadness came again. I saw me. I saw Simone, and I saw the gun.

"Your father would have done the same for me," she said.

"He still loves you," I said as I thought about the look in my father's eyes every time he mentioned her name.

"Simone loves you, Devlin," she said.

"I don't want to go back."

Before I could say another word, we were both back on the quilt, sitting in silence, watching the little girl play at the pond.

"When you were just a baby, I could see the determination in your eyes. You were destined for not only success, but for the love she has for you. Simone loves you."

"I want to stay here with you, with Grammy, with Jacob," I said.

"You can't stay, Devlin."

"Why not?" I asked.

"You have more life to live. You have people there that love you, that need you."

"I need you, Mama," I continued. I wanted her to let me stay.

She brought me into her bosom and hugged me tight. A hug let me know that this was not our last time together. I looked up at her and felt as if I were a child again. As if I were two years old again.

As we let go of our embrace, I noticed the little girl was hiding behind her.

"Hello," I said, attempting for the fourth time to speak to her.

"Hello," she finally responded.

"What's your name?"

"I don't have a name," she said with a smile.

"Everyone has a name."

My mother looked at the two of us and smiled. She kissed me on the cheek and did the same to the little girl before emerging from the moving quilt. As she stood and watched the little girl playing patty-cake, I felt a great peace. It was time for me to go back, but I was still scared, still afraid to go back to the unknown.

"Do I have to go back now?" I asked.

"Yes, Punkin', it's time."

"Living ain't easy, Mama," I said, thinking about the song Grammy always sang.

"But it's not yet your time to die," she said as she watched the little girl grab my hand.

I took one moment to look down at the little girl and when I looked back up, my mother was gone.

The little girl left the quilt and walked back over to the pond. Once she reached the bank, she summoned me to follow. This time I actually moved. Once I reached the pond, I stood beside the little girl and she pulled me down to her and gave me a hug.

"See you later, Daddy," she said as she gave me a kiss on my cheek.

"His eyes are open!" I heard someone yell.

My head was throbbing hard and the noise made it worse.

Suddenly, I saw several faces surrounding me.

"Mr. Carter, my name is Dr. Itu. Can you hear me?"

I was groggy and somewhat confused as I tried to focus on the person talking to me.

"Yes. I can hear you," I said as I tried to clear my throat.

A nurse placed a straw in my mouth.

"Do you recognize anyone in this room?" the doctor asked me after taking his flashlight out of my eyes.

I looked around slowly. I saw my father and Stephanie and I saw Reverend Jackson. I shook my head yes.

I began to search the room for Simone, but I did not see her. The last thing I remembered was seeing the window of the car come down and a gun stick out of the window. I wondered whether she was okay. Did the person that was shooting at her come back and get her? I needed to see her. I needed to know she was okay, but she was nowhere in view.

I thought about my dreams while I was in the coma. The conversations seemed so real. The emotions were deep. I felt Jacob, I felt Grammy, and I felt my mama. To me, it felt more than real.

After a few moments, the doctor excused himself to everyone to run some tests.

"You have a loving family," Dr. Itu said. "They all have been here since you were admitted last Thursday morning."

"What day is today?" I asked.

"It's a beautiful Sunday morning," he responded with a huge smile.

As he finished up, I heard the door open. It was Simone. She looked as if she had cried an ocean of tears. She seemed to be afraid to come in.

"Come on in, Ms. Jackson. I know you guys have a lot to talk about," the doctor said gleefully.

As she walked over to the side of the bed, I noticed the swells of her eyes. I could tell that she had little sleep and not much to eat.

She sat in the chair, not saying a word. As soon as Dr. Itu left, Simone began to cry. She finally left her chair and came closer to me.

"Devlin, I'm so—"

"Shh," I said.

"What do we do now?" she asked as she grabbed my hand.

"What we planned to do all along," I said, never more sure about anything in my life.

"I have something to tell you," she said, once again appearing to be nervous.

"You're having our baby," I said, already knowing what she was going to say.

She gave me a look of surprise, wondering how I knew.

"You're my Nina Mosley."

"And you, you're my Darius Lovehall," she said through her tears.

# *Sinful Ways*

As she drove down I-85 South, headed toward Atlanta, she realized that the life she once knew was now no more. Her plan, her plot, had executed perfectly until the end.

As she drove in silence, Leslie thought about the day that would change her life forever.

"Where is he going at this time of night?" she asked herself as she sat in the rented car strategically parked up the street from Devlin's house.

She knew something was going on with him. She had a feeling that someone else had moved into her space in his life, and she was going to find out who it was.

She did not follow too closely, and by the time she reached his destination, he had already entered the two-story house in the affluent neighborhood.

She rode around the neighborhood for hours, hoping to get a glimpse. The next morning, she decided to ride back by.

"Who is this bitch?" she asked herself aloud as she sat

in the driveway of the unknown woman's house. She got out of the car and began to look around the house to get some clues, but she found nothing.

Leslie rang the doorbell with the hopes of confronting this woman to let her know that she was wasting her time. Devlin was hers and she refused to let him go easily. But no one answered the door. As she was about to leave, she noticed a FedEx truck pull to the side of the house.

When the driver stepped out of his truck, she remained at the door. She slowly walked toward the delivery guy, acting as if it was a package for her.

"You're not Simone Jackson," the delivery guy said.

*Simone Jackson*, Leslie thought to herself. *He's seeing that black bitch?*

"Uhh. I am her new assistant. She asked me to meet you here. She's been waiting for this package."

At first, he gave her a look of suspicion. He had delivered several packages in the past, and he normally left them in her assigned spot.

Once he drove away, she noticed the sender's name on the package: Trinity Waters.

Back at her house, she quickly opened the package. Inside she found a dress and a letter.

*Dearest Simone,*

*How do I say what I feel? I am angry. I am sad. But most of all I am glad. I knew for ages now that you and I were only two ships passing only for a moment at sea. You never looked at me beyond the moments we shared, but it was my desire that you would eventually have the love for me that I have for you.*

*I learned a long time ago that we cannot force love on anyone. I think it would be best that from this point on we severed all ties. I wish you well with your show going national, and I wish you well with all your other endeavors.*

*Yours truly,*

*T.*

*P.S. Please don't call. I will no longer accept calls from you. Not because I'm angry, but because it would pain me to hear your voice.*

Leslie read the letter and reread the letter repeatedly to make sure she completely understood what it was she had read.

"Devlin's falling in love with a dyke." She laughed, but it immediately turned into sadness, then sudden anger.

After several shots of Jamaican rum, she felt an urge of vindictiveness run through her body. She grabbed a pair of scissors and furiously cut the dress in pieces. Once she finished, she looked at the pile of cloth that lay on her floor. She found an old box in her closet and placed the torn dress inside.

"Devlin is mine," she said as she drove to the FedEx office to have them deliver the package to Simone at the studio.

Days had gone by and she had to come up with a plan. After her last visit to Devlin's house, she saw in his eyes that he was done with her and her lies. She thought about the day she used the key she had to Devlin's house, the one he never knew she had, and began to look around his house. She had no idea what she was looking for, but found something that caused her to become angry with him: his grandmother's Bible.

She had walked into her room, the only room that she had never been in all the years she had known him. After seeing the Bible sitting there, something led her to open it, where she discovered a white envelope addressed to a

Henry Carlisle. She carefully opened the envelope and read the letter.

"If you had informed me of your inheritance in the beginning, we would all be happy now," she said as she continued down the highway.

"Just a casualty of war," she said softly to herself after a brief thought of Trinity.

She was an innocent victim. Leslie knew that Trinity was able to do what she could not do, what she had refused to do, and that was to move on.

Leslie thought about all the years she wanted, yet never had. She thought about her struggles as a child wanting the things her mother could not afford. Yes, she wanted love, but love could not afford her the happiness she desired, or at least she thought it could not.

"Trinity," the strongly accented voice answered when she called.

"Hello, Trinity, my name is Victoria Thompson," Leslie said to her the first time they held a conversation over the phone.

"How can I help you, Ms. Thompson?"

"I am in need of a stylist," Leslie said, creating a lie to get in close.

She knew what she had to do during her first visit to LA. A lesbian affair was nothing new to her. She had been this route before. She did not mind doing what she had to do to get what she wanted.

She thought about the many nights she lay with Trinity, fuming because she knew Simone was with Devlin. She thought about the four of them, all connecting to form a strange puzzle.

"Did you love her?" Leslie asked Trinity one night, after Trinity confided in her about her past relations with Simone.

"Yes. I still have a love for her," Trinity had said in her thickly accented voice. "But sometimes, when you love, you have to let go."

Leslie refused to let go. She was on a mission to reclaim what was rightfully hers.

She was in some part of South Carolina when she stopped to get gas. As she walked out of the station, she noticed the headlines of the newspaper.

Devlin Carter, fiancé to talk show host Simone Jackson, shot in driveway of his home.

She stared long and hard at the headlines, realizing that it was not supposed to happen this way. "He wasn't supposed to save her," she said to herself. "He wasn't supposed to save her."

Her plan was perfect. The phone calls, the threats, the dead rat, the video that she found once while visiting Trinity. Killing Trinity to make her look like the scorned lover was supposed to make Devlin come back. As she stared at the newspaper headlines, she thought of her plan, how it was supposed to work, and how it failed.

It was not hard to get Trinity to fly to Charlotte. Trinity had fallen for her, had trusted her, but little did Trinity realize that the trust would eventually kill her.

She watched Devlin from across the street when he arrived home to see the package in his door. She waited, and then called Simone. She knew Devlin would be angry. She knew he would be hurt from seeing it, but she also knew that she could be the one to help in his time of hurt.

As she watched Devlin and Simone standing on the porch, she waited. She noticed that Devlin looked toward her. At first she thought he saw her, but the windows were tinted, and he could not see who was inside the car.

As she slowly drove by the third time, she noticed Devlin walking back toward his house. She stopped, and as quickly as she pulled the trigger, Devlin had jumped in front of Simone. Leslie's heart dropped when she saw the man that she loved lying on the ground. She sped off.

Two hours later, she was in downtown Charlotte on the top floor of a parking deck, waiting on Trinity. She parked her Mercedes a few feet away from the Chevy Caprice. Once Trinity arrived in a rental car, Leslie got out of her car and walked toward her.

"Why are we meeting here, love?" Trinity asked as she looked at Leslie's hands. "And why are you wearing gloves in the summer?"

Leslie had no words for her. She grabbed her hand and led her toward the driver's side of the Caprice. Then she passionately kissed Trinity.

"Kinky," Trinity said with a seductive smile, not realizing she was moments away from death.

As they embraced again, Leslie pulled the gun out that she had stuck under her overly large shirt, and without any hesitation, pulled the trigger.

She then quickly placed a similar pair of gloves on Trinity's hands, and swiftly left in her Mercedes, leaving Trinity's memory on this earth as a vindictive lover.

"Dead rats die unnoticed," she said aloud as she drove away.

She knew her life was now different and that she could not remain in Charlotte. She had to leave immediately. She drove two hours before stopping at a cheap hotel on I-85 South to Atlanta. After taking a quick shower and changing clothes, she returned to the highway unsure of what her next move would be.

* * *

A couple of hours later, she found herself sitting in a hotel room in Atlanta. She thought about her life. She thought about the love she still had for a man who risked his life for another woman. She thought about her actions over the past several months. Everything she had done, the lies, the deceit, the murder, were all her sinful ways.

## Book Club Discussion Questions

1. Do you believe that Leslie truly loved Devlin, or was she more in love with money?
2. Did Trinity deserve the treatment given to her by Simone?
3. What were your initial thoughts when Henry revealed to Devlin who he was?
4. Why do you think Simone refused to reveal her past to Devlin?
5. Devlin experienced loss throughout his life. Did his loss weaken him or make him strong?
6. What were your overall thoughts of the relationship Simone had with her parents?
7. How did you feel about Jacob?
8. When Simone received the dead rat, what were your initial thoughts about Trinity?
9. How surprised were you with the ending? Did you predict it?
10. Is there any character(s) from *Livin' Ain't Easy* you would like to see again?

Coming Soon . . .

# The First Person

# 1

# *T'Shobi Wells*

I looked over at the clock, pissed that I had allowed myself to fall asleep. Justine was supposed to have been gone a long time ago. As a matter of fact, she wasn't supposed to be there at all.

Ordinarily, my rule was not to allow into my humble abode anyone that didn't call first. But, I allowed her to get away with breaking that rule far too many times, and regardless of how many times I reminded her, she still chose to do things in her own way.

When I got up from my bed, I heard the vibration of my phone going off for the umpteenth time. I didn't bother to look to see who it was. I already knew. My plans for the evening were drastically delayed, and there was no need to look at my missed calls or to listen to the voice mail messages that would only remind me of where I was supposed to be.

"Justine," I said as I gently nudged her. "It's almost twelve o'clock. You need to get up now. I'm sure Pastor Reynolds is wondering where his wife is."

"Fuck him," she mumbled. "His tired ass is probably somewhere with one of his *tricks*."

"Seriously, Justine, I don't think that it's cool for you to stay out so late. I'm almost certain that he's worried sick about you."

She finally began to move around under the sheets, while continuing to mumble curses. As I watched her naked body emerge from the bed, I couldn't help but notice how perfect it was for her to be a mature woman with two adult children and three grandchildren.

Her honey-colored, flawless skin was immaculate, and her body could compete and win any day against any young woman in her early twenties. The first day I met her, all I could think of was how much she reminded me of Phylicia Rashad.

In my twenty-seven years on earth, I had never dated or had sex with a woman my age or younger. I'd always been attracted to older women. I knew it partly stemmed from the fact that my mother was never a major part of my life. I tried not to get into all the psychoanalytical bullshit, but I realized that her giving me up at an early age and my once strong desire to find motherly love had a lot to do with it.

"I'm not sure if I like the fact that you are kicking me out of your apartment, T'Shobi. This is the third time in a row," she said as she walked out of the bathroom. "I'm beginning to think that you and that damn Tinisha Jackson really are having a thing. Don't think that I don't hear the little rumors floating around the church."

I stood silent as she spoke. I had heard the rumors too, but that's all they were. Tinisha was three years younger than I was, and nowhere near my flavor of loving.

"Justine, you know those are just lies. Since coming to New Deliverance Church as the minister of music, there's only been one woman that I've been with or even desired to be with."

I walked toward her, wrapped my arms around that perfect body of hers, and allowed my lips to touch hers.

"Um-huh, and it better stay that way too."

After walking Justine to her car, I literally ran back to my room and checked my cell phone.

Sixteen missed calls, ten messages on my voice mail, and five text messages. I already knew who it was. I decided to take a long, hot shower before calling back to inform that I was on the way.

While the hot water splashed across my body, I thought about my life over the past year. I had moved from Atlanta, Georgia to Charlotte, North Carolina hoping to escape my past, but as always, my ways never allowed me to get as far as I wanted to or as far as I needed to.

I thought of the words MeeMa had spoken the day I left Montgomery, Alabama nine years earlier: "Baby, no matter how far you run away, you will never be able to run from yourself." Even if I didn't want to admit it, I knew she told me nothing but the truth.

My MeeMa was a wise old woman who took me in as her own when I was sixteen. She was the one that taught me how to live and even love again after all the bullshit I had experienced in my short years of living.

When I walked back into my bedroom, I heard my phone singing the distinctive ring tone, once again informing me of how late I was.

"I'm about twenty minutes away," I said, then hung up without waiting for a response.

Driving in my car, I thought about the first time I met Justine Reynolds, the First Lady of New Deliverance Church. She walked into Pastor Reynolds's office without knocking.

"I'm sorry, Seth. I didn't realize you were meeting with someone." Her voice was melodic, sounding as if she were singing.

"Sweetheart," he began as he rose from his desk, "please come in and allow me to introduce you to our possible new minister of music, T'Shobi Wells."

"Oh, this is the infamous Mr. Wells. I must tell you, I've heard nothing but great things about you. If all is true, I can't wait to see how you turn our music ministry around."

Pastor Reynolds and I continued discussing my duties and compensation, while Justine pranced around the office as if she were cleaning up and making sure everything was in place.

It was difficult for me not to notice her, and I could tell that she was checking me out as well. I've always had a gift of knowing when someone wanted to sex me. I've been a musician for churches as well as in the music industry for years, and for some reason, I was always a target for older women. I had my very first sexual encounter with an older woman at ten, and as I got older, I learned how to decipher certain looks and innuendos, a gift that was also a dreaded curse.

When Pastor Reynolds and I completed our conversation, I decided to attend services the following Sunday to get a feel for how things were there, as well as a feel for his congregation.

Once I drove into the parking lot, the first person I noticed was Justine. She damned near broke a heel flagging me down to instruct me that I could park my car in front of the sign that read MINISTER OF MUSIC.

I locked the door of my BMW and she immediately placed her arm inside of mine and escorted me toward the front door.

"I see playing keyboards has been good to you," she said, looking back and admiring my car.

"It's been a blessing."

"Well, I'm sure you will find it a blessing if you decide to rest your magic fingers here at New Deliverance." She gave me the most sensuous smile, and I could actually feel my southern region begin to move.

When we walked into the church, all eyes looked toward her as she escorted me to the front of the church where the musicians sat. By the jealous look I received from the keyboardist who they had been using in the interim, I could tell he wanted to kick my ass, but Justine quickly shooed him away as if he were a small child in the way.

"I can't wait to see what those magic hands can do," she said with a wink before taking her rightful seat on the front row.

When service was over, Pastor Reynolds invited me over to their house for dinner. As I sat at the table with their two grown sons, their wives and children, I could feel Justine's eyes piercing my skin. I did my best to avoid eye contact with her, but she made it impossible. Every time she spoke, her question or topic of conversation was directed to me.

It was difficult, trying not to notice her, but I did. She was exactly the type of woman that had always turned me on. She was mature, yet had the energy of a teenager. Her hair was short, black, and had just a hint of gray that made her look distinguished, and as I said before, she had the body that could make any man shout hallelujah.

For weeks after accepting the job, I pleaded with myself not to take things to a sexual level with her, but as all temptations seem to do, it took over like a raging bull. One week, five days, twelve hours, and fifty-two minutes of trying to hold out from her had caved in.

When I arrived at the hotel, thoughts of what happened when I was in Atlanta replayed in my head. Being in a similar situation was the reason I left. I wanted to start fresh. I wanted to start new. I thought I could do that by leaving Atlanta, but as the months passed, I realized that it wasn't Atlanta that I had to run from; it was me that needed to change.

Riding on the elevator of the Blake Hotel in uptown Charlotte, my mind quickly traveled back to that first dinner at Pastor Seth and Justine Reynolds's home. She wasn't the only one checking me out that day. She wasn't the only one telling me with their eyes what they wanted to do to me or have me do to them.

"Why the fuck do I continue to do these things?" I asked myself softly as I stepped off the elevator.

When I arrived to the room, I tapped lightly on the door.

"About damn time. What in hell took you so long?"

"I'm sorry. I got tied up with something," I said as we embraced.

"Tied up with something, or with someone? The rumor is that you and that cute little girl Tinisha Jackson have a thing going on."

"Seth, you should know better than anyone that Tinisha Jackson is definitely not my flavor," I responded to Pastor Seth Reynolds as we fell onto the bed to make love until the early hours of the morning.